Dear Mom and Dad, Don't Worry

Dear Mom and Dad, Don't Worry

Carol Snyder

BANTAM BOOKS
NEW YORK · TORONTO · LONDON · SYDNEY · AUCKLAND

DEAR MOM AND DAD, DON'T WORRY
A Bantam Book / November 1989

*The Starfire logo is a registered trademark of Bantam Books, a
division of Bantam Doubleday Dell Publishing Group, Inc.
Registered in U.S. Patent and Trademark Office and elsewhere.*

Library of Congress Cataloging-in-Publication Data

Snyder, Carol.
Dear Mom and Dad, don't worry.

Summary: When thirteen-year-old Carly finds herself in the
hospital with a fractured spine and discovers that she will have
to wear a brace to walk again, her condition helps her put her
other problems in a different perspective.
[1. Wounds and injuries—Fiction.   2. Self-perception—Fiction]
I. Title.
PZ7.S68517De   1989   [Fic]   89–15063
ISBN 0-553-05801-0

Published simultaneously in the United States and Canada

---

*Bantam Books are published by Bantam Books, a division of Bantam
Doubleday Dell Publishing Group, Inc. Its trademark, consisting of the
words "Bantam Books" and the portrayal of a rooster, is Registered in U.S.
Patent and Trademark Office and in other countries. Marca Registrada.
Bantam Books, 666 Fifth Avenue, New York, New York 10103.*

PRINTED IN THE UNITED STATES OF AMERICA

FG   0 9 8 7 6 5 4 3 2 1

To Marsha Cohen Rifkin
always my friend
since age two—
who shares my
respect for hammocks
and is not to blame.

Dear Mom and Dad, Don't Worry

APRIL

Chapter One

Don't Ask for Trouble

My mind was made up on two subjects I never even thought I'd ever have to think about. One, I, Carly Stern, age thirteen, will never use this bedpan, no matter how desperate I get. Two, I will not let anyone know how scared I am. Especially my parents. They have enough to worry about.

Where was that doctor, anyway? He'd better let me get up. How many hours had passed since I'd said good-bye to my mother? My mouth felt dry and my head felt as if it were full of cotton balls. I guess it was the medication. What was I still doing here? I thought I was only going to the hospital for X rays. I wished there were a phone in the room. I'd call my best friend, Michelle. After all, what are best friends for? I remembered the nurse's telling me not to move or I could cause damage. My mother warned me, too:

"Please, Carly. Do what the doctors and nurses say. You're injured. Don't ask for trouble." I wasn't asking for trouble. But I had more than my share of it.

The room was dark. What time was it? This doctor had better get his act together and get on the job. I had

French homework to do for school tomorrow. True, I'd left it till the last minute, but I expected to have all evening to do it. Mme. Larson doesn't accept excuses.

I saw out of the corner of my eye that Tina, my gray-haired roommate, was asleep. I heard her snoring. I was afraid to move anything but my eyes. Everyone was scaring me to death. I felt if I made one little move I'd never walk again. I pushed that thought out of my mind. It was too scary to think about.

I saw the glass of water with a straw in it close by on the nightstand. Why couldn't I just reach over and help myself? I like taking care of myself. I'm an independent daughter. I thought about the crazy work hours my parents put in at their men's clothing store. When would they visit me? Where were they now when I needed them? I tried to raise my hand, but it felt like lead. Too much medication, I thought. Where were those nurses now when I wanted a drink of water? I didn't want to call out and wake my roommate. If I could pull the cord by my bed, a light would be turned on at the nurses' station. But what if I couldn't pull it?

If I could just get the guardrail down and move so that I could swing over the side of my bed, I could find a bathroom like a normal human being *and* get a drink of water. I heard my mother's voice in my head. "Don't ask for trouble."

I dozed again. When I opened my eyes, it was light. Tina was still asleep.

"So how was your night?" a nurse asked, laughing as she popped a thermometer in my mouth. "How are you supposed to answer when I just stuck a thermometer in your mouth, right? By the way, my name is Judy."

I smiled, thermometer and all, then mumbled, "I'm not here with chicken pox or the flu. What's with the thermometer?"

"It's one of the standard rules," Judy answered, removing the thermometer. "It's routine every time we change shifts. Now I'm going to take your pulse and get you all freshened up." She closed the curtains and started giving me a sponge bath. She swished a washrag around in a container of water. I was dying of shyness and embarrassment. I tried to make believe this wasn't happening to me.

"Do you like school or hate school?" she asked. "What grade are you in?"

"Eighth grade. Usually, I don't mind school," I chattered as if this were an ordinary conversation. "I get good marks and I have a lot of friends, but I can't stand my French class. I love the language, but I hate the way my teacher embarrasses kids and makes fun of how they say things."

"School can be rough," Judy said sympathetically. "Do you have a boyfriend?" she asked, drying me off.

I pictured myself fully dressed and talked full speed to hide my embarrassment. "Not really. Well, there's a boy I like from school. He asked me to a party recently, but I had to say no because I was going with my family to our summer house at the lake. My parents wanted to get away and relax for spring vacation. Some relaxation. I end up in the hospital and—" A shooting pain went through me and I gasped.

5

"Easy does it," Judy said. The pain stopped but my stomach turned over with fear. It was hard to push the fear out of my mind, but I went on talking as if nothing were wrong.

"I'm afraid the boy I like probably thinks I don't like him."

"You'll have lots of boyfriends soon enough," Judy said. "Now, Carly, sooner or later you're going to have to face the dreaded moment of that bedpan or you're going to float away or have your bladder emptied with a tube. The outflow column on your chart is empty. I'll get the bedpan. You'll have privacy." She ducked out of the curtain not waiting for me to refuse. Suddenly the curtain swung open before I could even grab for the sheet to cover myself. I looked up expecting to see Judy.

Instead I stared up at big brown eyes in a suntanned face. "I'm Dr. Ginario," a low-pitched, confident voice said.

"Haven't you ever heard of knocking?" I answered, covering myself as best I could. "How could you just fling the curtain open?" A wave of anger felt better than fear. I wanted to scream at everyone. Why had this happened to me? What *had* happened to me?

The doctor closed the curtain and called, "Doctors are used to seeing patients unclothed but I'll give you a few minutes to compose yourself and come back. We can start over again."

Judy returned, and without asking any questions she stuck the cold metal pan under my rear, pulled the sheet up over me, and in my hand placed a half-filled glass of water with a straw that bent until it reached my mouth. "Sip slowly and your body will take care of itself," she said, and vanished.

When I'd taken care of that business, Dr. Ginario returned. He pulled the curtain closed after he stepped up to the bed.

"Hello, Carly," he said as if meeting me for the first time. "I'm Dr. Ginario."

I looked into his eyes. They glistened with such seriousness as he talked to me. My heart started to pound with fear. "I've studied your X rays. Are your parents here?"

"No. My dad isn't all that comfortable in hospitals and my mom took him home. She'll be back. She's bringing me a robe and slippers and stuff. I'll be going home now, right?"

"I usually talk to the parents first," Dr. Ginario said, "but you're not a child. I also believe the patient should know what's going on. I'm afraid you won't be going home so soon."

My heart started to beat even faster. "What do you mean?" I asked. "What's wrong with me?"

"You've fractured your spine," Dr. Ginario explained, his voice trying to be kind. "Your first and second vertebrae, the bones you feel in your spinal column, are compressed, smashed together. And your third vertebra is fractured, cracked. What happened to you? An automobile accident? Fall off a horse?"

My tongue stopped working. Fractured vertebra? Was that another way to say broken back?

"Well, actually," I stalled, to catch my breath. I felt like a real jerk. "I fell off a hammock, only about two feet to the ground when the cord broke." It sounded so stupid to me that I decided I'd better work on a better explanation, such as, I had a flying accident.

"It's the way a person falls, not how far," Dr. Ginario said. "You will have to lie flat on your back for two to three weeks while the bones are healing and while we have you fitted with a back brace. I don't even want to move you to examine you. I just want to see if you can wiggle your toes. Can you do that for me now?" he asked. He walked to the foot of my bed.

I thought I wiggled my toes. It felt as if I wiggled them just fine, but I couldn't see and he didn't say anything more about it. He just looked very worried, as if I hadn't.

"Do you have any questions?" he asked, standing next to me again.

I wanted to ask if my toes wiggled, but I guess I was afraid to know the answer. Instead I said, "Yes. You will tell the nurse I can get up to go to the bathroom, won't you?"

"That would be very dangerous for you now," he explained. "For the first few days especially, any movement can cause more damage. You must protect the nerves in and around your spinal cord. The orderlies will be bringing a board to slip under your mattress to make it firmer. But, on the brighter side, at least you don't seem to need any surgery or traction *for now*. You can turn your head from side to side and use your arms, but even that, do slowly and carefully."

I could hear my heart pounding. He was so serious. I was too frightened to ask anything more. I decided to imagine that my toes had wiggled just fine and he couldn't possibly know what he was talking about. Did no surgery *now* mean maybe surgery later? I didn't want to know.

"You'll have some medication to keep you relaxed," he said, "and if you work with me on this, there's an excellent chance you'll recover quickly."

"I'll be here awhile longer so I can speak to your mother. Then she'll probably want to go home to get some rest, because you'll be asleep from the medication. I'll see you tomorrow," he said, and stepped outside the curtain.

"Dr. Ginario. Could you open the curtain?" I asked.

"Sure," he said, and pulled it open.

I was so nervous I decided it would be best not to think about myself. I'd keep my mind busy looking at my new environment. I started with Dr. Ginario. As he turned away, I noticed he didn't wear a wedding ring. He was really cute. Maybe he'd end up on my most-romantic-couples list that I was making with my friend Michelle, but paired with whom? The thought relaxed me a bit. I wished Michelle were here to take my mind off my pain and worry. Would I ever wiggle my toes and get out of bed?

Of all the lake-house dangers Mom and Dad were always harping on, no one had ever warned me about hammocks. Who'd have thought a material swing would be the cause of a broken back? I was so angry, and there was no one to blame but myself.

Chapter Two

You Have to Take
the Bad With the Good

The clatter of breakfast trays woke me up. I saw a nurse's aide placing a steaming bowl on the table next to my pillow. She smiled and said, "Oatmeal."

"Yuck," I answered.

"She can't sit up to feed herself," my roommate instructed the aide. "She'll need some help."

"Well, of course," the aide said, placing a large square of blue plastic under my chin. She put the bowl on top of my chest, a spoon in my right hand, and my left hand around the bowl. I struggled to get a spoonful from the bowl to my mouth without its oozing down my chin. What if I had to eat like that for the rest of my life? That awful thought sent a painful chill up my spine.

"You're not actually going to eat that slop, are you?" Tina asked.

"No," I said. "Two spoonfuls were enough. One more and the sides of my throat will be pasted together."

Tina laughed and said, "Let me handle this. Nurse," she called, and the aide reappeared. "Do us all a favor before that kid chokes. Save the porridge for Goldi-locks and bring her some cut-up French toast drenched in syrup. And bring me some, too. It's the only thing in this joint worth eating in the morning. Trust me, Carly," she said, turning to me.

The nurse's aide chuckled as she removed the cereal bowls. "Goldilocks," I heard her say. A few minutes later she returned with French toast swimming in sweet syrup—soggy with it. Mine was all cut up. "I have permission to crank your bed up a bit so you can swallow better," she said.

I ate a piece of French toast. Every taste made me think of my mother. She makes the best French toast with thick challah bread. Why wasn't she here to comfort me? I want my mother, I cried to myself. I want her here with me right now. I'm frightened. I want to be home in Brooklyn in my pink bedroom. I felt empty inside, then angry.

"Do you know what time it is?" I asked Tina.

"Let's see," she said, reaching with her good hand and opening the drawer of her night table. She took out a wristwatch. "Seven thirty-five."

"It's only seven thirty-five and we're cleaned up and finished with breakfast already? How long till visiting hours?"

"Visiting hours are from two to four and six to eight," she said. "So we've got plenty of time to get to know each other. That's all there is to do in hospitals. Get to know people and think. It's the same in my bar and grill. You learn a lot about life thinking and listen-ing to people."

Six and one half hours more about Tina's life was more than I wanted to know, I thought. She looked about sixty. Why wasn't I in a room with a kid my own age? Someone who would understand. I wanted Michelle or Mom and Dad. I wanted to ask why the doctor was so serious when he asked me if I could wiggle my toes. I wanted to know why this had to happen to me.

"Doesn't this hospital even have phones in the room or remote control TVs?" I asked.

"There's a phone in every hall," Tina answered, "and I'm on the waiting list for a TV that works. Your parents can get a phone installed for you if the doctor says you can have one."

"No phone. That's the worst," I said. "I've never in my entire life been without a phone. I can't even sit up, still less get up and walk to a hall phone. It's not fair."

"True, but that's life. What's your philosophy of life?" she asked, and then added, "That's a thoughtful question to keep you busy!"

"I don't have one," I said.

"You don't have a philosophy?" she said with surprise. "You must have your own ideas which get you from day to day and through tough times. Here's one of my favorites. I've been in and out of this hospital ever since I fell on the ice and broke my elbow," Tina went on. "I've had the bone set, broken, and reset with a pin, which meant surgery."

"That sounds painful," I said.

"The words that got me through all this misery were, 'This too shall pass.' And speaking of passing, when you gotta go, you gotta go," she said, and shuffled to the bathroom.

"Wish I could do that. Just going to the bathroom now is going to be an event. I've always done things for myself. I've always done things for everybody else, too. When the phone rings at home, I'm the one who gets it. I never walk. I run. Till now, anyway."

"Patience," Tina called. "You gotta learn to have patience. I'll be right back."

Two men in white came in struggling with a big board.

"This two oh six?" the taller one asked.

"This is two oh six," the second man said with authority.

"This board's for you," the taller man said.

"Take care, kid, you hear?" the shorter orderly said. "Sometimes things seem worse than they are."

"Thanks," I said. It seemed as if everyone dished out philosophy.

Tina went for her "constitutional," as she called walking up and down the hall, and Judy came in to give me some medication, which made me drowsy. I yawned and drifted off to sleep. It was lunchtime when I woke up.

"Wait until you see this feast," Tina's voice greeted me, and I saw she was dangling her feet over the side of her bed and picking at something on her plate, the way crows pick on something dead. "They put this gravy on top so you can't tell what it is you're eating," she complained. "I'm gonna tell my husband, Leo, to heat up some veal Parmesan from the freezer and bring it for us. Then when everyone leaves tonight, you and I will have a party."

Tina rang for the nurse. One, with hair as white as her uniform, came in to help me with lunch. She insisted on feeding me, but her hands were shaky. I ended up with more noodles slithering down the side of my neck than down my throat.

Where were my mother and father? I got what felt like a hole in my stomach. What if I couldn't walk again and for the rest of my life I had to wait. Wait for my mother to bathe me or for my father to bring me food or take me outside in a wheelchair. And I'd see people stare at me like I've stared at people on crutches. They wouldn't see me. They'd just see what was wrong with me. I pictured my friends turning away, embarrassed to be with me. I started to shake and feel nauseated.

"What's the matter, Carly?" Tina asked. "You've turned white as a sheet. Was it the food?" She struggled over, only able to use one hand to pull a chair up beside me. She sat down, reached over, and took my hand in hers. "Your hand is ice-cold, but you're sweating. Poor baby, you're scared to death, aren't you. Trying not to let on but imagining all kinds of horrible things. I know. I've felt that way. It's no crime. I understand." She rubbed my hand so gently as she spoke. I turned my head toward the wall so Tina wouldn't see the tear that had escaped. I'd promised myself that I wouldn't let anyone know how scared I was and I didn't let her know. But she knew anyway... and cared.

"I feel like I'm in the middle of a three-tissue movie," I said.

"Sure, sweetie." She laughed. "Here's a tissue."

Finally it was visiting hours. I listened to people arriving and asking room directions from the head nurse at the station just outside my door. Mom and Dad would be the first ones there; I just knew they probably arrived early. Every minute past two o'clock seemed like an hour. I lay still listening for their footsteps.

I asked Tina for a time check every five minutes. "Relax," she said, "they'll be here. They probably stopped to speak to the doctor."

At three o'clock the elevator door squealed open and I recognized the footsteps. Soon I felt Mom's lips on my forehead and her finger stroking my hair. "Hi, sweetie," she said.

I closed my eyes, feeling a sense of relief at her tender touch. I wasn't alone anymore. My family is here, I thought. I would be all right. But I couldn't hide my feelings. "Where have you been? What took you so long? I waited and waited." Tears long held back started trickling out of the corners of my eyes. I stiffened to gain control and got a shooting pain.

"I'm here now," Mom said. "I've been waiting in Dr. Ginario's office. They felt it would be best if I let you rest until visiting hours. And two-forty was exactly when Dr. Ginario got out of surgery and stopped to talk to me. Did you have a good night?"

I thought of my promise to myself not to let anyone know how scared I was and cause them to worry. I couldn't speak yet. I answered her question in my mind.

On a score of one to ten, the first night of my life spent alone in a hospital was not one that I could call good. A scary night, yes. An uncomfortable night, definitely. "Good" did not have anything to do with it. But I could see the hopefulness in Mom's eyes. I swallowed my feelings and said, "I gave it a five. It was okay. Where's Daddy?" I asked, realizing I hadn't been greeted by him.

Mom looked uncomfortable. "You know Daddy and his hospital phobia. He just couldn't come in. He made it to the elevator door and then he had to leave. He sends his love and says he's waiting in the car but he's thinking of you. He said he'll try again tomorrow."

"Couldn't he just come up and say hello even if his stomach does flips?" I asked. How could a father, my father, not be beside me at a time like this?

"Can I get you anything?" Mom changed the subject.

"Yeah. You can get me out of here. Ma, I can't just lie here and miss all the work at school and not even have a phone."

"I know this is rough on you, Carly. It's rough on all of us. We just have to be strong and take the bad with the good."

"Is that your philosophy?" I asked.

"I suppose you could call it that." Then she asked me the question that seemed so simple but which sent chills through me. "Can you wiggle your toes today?"

Chapter Three

Everything in Life Is Not Fair

On Tuesday of my first week in the hospital, Tina came back from one of her constitutionals and said, "I've got the perfect guy for you. He's gorgeous. Big blue eyes. Reddish hair. Your all-American look. You better stop feeling sorry for yourself and perk up. I invited him to visit."

"I've never looked so bad in my life," I said. Tina handed me my brush and mirror. "Thanks," I said, "but it won't help. My hair needs to be washed. It's changed from shiny brown to dull brown."

"Tell your mother to bring you that dry shampoo, the one you brush into your hair," Tina suggested.

If I had a phone, I could catch Mom at the store and she could bring my dry shampoo tonight at visiting hours.

"On my next walk, I'll call your mother for you," Tina interrupted my thoughts.

"Thanks, anyway," I said. "But I don't want to bother her. My parents have a lot on their minds. They may have to move out of their store, and as if that's not enough, my sister's having problems with her husband. My dad's phobia gets worse each time he tries to visit me. And here I am miles away from the city so they have to commute each evening to see me and feel guilty for not being here in the afternoon. I feel so sorry for them."

"They sure have their hands full," Tina said. "At least now you admit you feel something, huh, Miss Stiff Upper Lip? I'll phone my husband, Leo, and tell him to bring you dry shampoo. He loves when he can help someone. Maybe because we never had any kids. We just baby each other." Tina glanced lovingly at the photo of Leo on her nightstand, then handed me a lipstick.

As I put it on, I moved the mirror just a bit, made a great discovery, and changed the subject. "Hey, Tina. Look. I can see everything that's going on in the hall. There's Dr. Ginario talking to Judy. They're looking at charts, but they're standing very close to each other. Do you think this could be the start of something?"

Observing took my mind off my own worries and fears. Dr. Ginario still says I don't need surgery and adds the scary word . . . *yet*.

A little boy walked into the room pulling a pole on wheels with IV bottles jingling. He looked about ten and had curly red hair.

"Jonathan," Tina said, "we'll have to get you some oil for those wheels. I want you to meet Carly." Then she turned to me and said, "This is the gorgeous guy I've been telling you about. Ha, ha. I really had you going there, didn't I?" We both laughed.

"We're not laughing at you, honey," Tina said to the

boy. "I just played a joke on Carly." Then she said, "Jonathan, do your impression of Mrs. Todd, the head nurse. Go ahead. Make Carly laugh like I do so she'll get better quicker."

Jonathan held his head high and puffed out his chest. "Visiting hours are now over. At the sound of the bell, all visitors are to leave *immediately*." He had that grouchy Mrs. Todd's voice down pat.

"Jonathan had an operation two weeks ago," Tina said after he left.

So on Thursday, when Tina came in and said, "There's a gorgeous guy for you" again, I paid no attention. I didn't comb my hair. I didn't put on lipstick or anything. Tina really set me up because in walked the hunk of the year. He was on crutches because his foot was in a cast, but he looked as if he were straight off one of those hunk calendars. I stared, following his every move. I got a funny feeling in my chest and I wanted him to come closer.

"How's my best girlfriend?" he said to Tina, and gave her a hug. "And who's that doll in the other bed?"

Some doll, I thought. I probably looked like a Cabbage Patch kid. Judy was going to dry shampoo my hair in a little while. Why couldn't this blond answer to a girl's dreams come in a little later? And why did I feel as if I might not be able to speak?

"Carly, say hello to Jess."

"Hello, Jess," I said finally, wanting to pull the blanket up over my head.

21

"Hey, Carly, what's a pretty girl like you doing in a dump like this?" Jess asked.

"It's a long story," I said.

"Go ahead. I've got time. Talk about it. I want to hear. You should talk about it. That's what the doctor told me about my motorcycle accident. You tell me your story, then I'll tell you mine. I'm all ears." Jess rested his crutches against a wall and pulled up a chair next to my bed. He straddled the chair so he was seated backward.

Jess was definitely not all ears. This close I could clearly see he was all muscle.

"Hit by a car?" he said, prompting me. I was temporarily speechless. "Football injury?" he teased, and I suddenly found myself teasing back. "Flying accident," I joked. "Actually, I flew out of a hammock. You really want to hear all the details? It's just so stupid."

"Accidents usually are stupid," he said. "That's why they're accidents. You don't plan them carefully."

"I've heard these stories already," Tina said, chasing an elusive slipper with her foot. "I'll leave you two to get to know each other and check out that old woman in two ten, the heart attack."

"Don't break any hearts along the way," Jess flirted.

As Tina walked by, I saw her reach over and gently smack Jess on the back. He made believe she'd hurt him.

"What a faker. Give the man an Academy Award." Tina didn't ever seem to miss a beat.

Jess smiled. "Alone at last. Now, shoot. Tell your flying hammock story."

"Okay, here goes." I started wondering if he could hear my pulse pounding. "My best friend, Michelle, came with my parents and me to our country house on the lake. The two of us decided to relax on the hammock. I hung the ropes from hooks on two trees and we both sat in it. Suddenly, Michelle's side collapsed and we were both on the ground giggling. Here's the stupid part. Since no one was hurt, we decided to try again. I tied a knot in the rope and we switched sides because I'm lighter. Just as I was going to sit down, my side collapsed and I flew out of the hammock." Jess was staring intently at me. I had to concentrate to finish my story. His eyes were so blue. "I couldn't brace my fall because I was on my way sitting down, so I fell very hard smack on my..." I stopped, searching for a way to put it.

"Your butt," Jess filled in the blank.

"You got it. I thought I was well padded, but I guess I'm not."

He laughed.

"Anyway, the fall knocked the wind out of me so I couldn't yell. Michelle was laughing and waiting for me to get up. When I didn't, she realized I was hurt and called my dad, who came running and started yelling at me for 'fooling around on the hammock in the first place.' Then it was like in some old speeded-up movie. My mother came yelling at my father for yelling at me when I was hurt."

"I can picture that," Jess said, and laughed.

"Our neighbor ran barefoot down the hill over all these rocks, and he helped my father carry me to the car. I thought I was only going to the hospital for X rays. It turned out—"

"'To make a long story short,' as my mother says," Jess interrupted, grinning.

"It turned out I have a fractured spine. My first and second vertebrae are compressed and my third is fractured." I didn't mention possible surgery.

"We make some odd couple," Jess said. "You with a broken back and me with a broken leg. How long do you have to be in bed?"

"I have to be flat on my back for two to three weeks, depending on when my brace is ready. Then I can sit up and hopefully walk again. I'll have to wear the brace for two months or more, depending. Dr. Ginario said I'm lucky, my toes are starting to wiggle." And I don't have to be in traction or have surgery, *at this time*, was the thought I buried again. "My friend Michelle feels really guilty," I said, trying to switch the conversation away from me. "She said she should have sat down first. It was on her side. She sends me get-well cards every day and signs them 'I'm sorry.' I wish she'd stop blaming herself. It wasn't her fault."

"It was your fault because you never were a Boy Scout or a sailor and never learned to tie knots," Jess said, then added, "Ginario's the best doctor. When I had to have my bone broken and reset, he did it, and I had other internal injuries, too. You will see that my accident did not show great intelligence, either. At least I was wearing a helmet. That saved my life."

"What happened?" I asked, feeling the tingly warmth of Jess's hand on mine.

"I was being a big shot and trying to do wheelies with a much too powerful set of wheels and engine under me," Jess explained. "I was obviously sitting on my brain at the time. The rest's history. Blood and gore and broken pieces."

"Very descriptive." I joked, "What's your sentence?"

"This place is like that prison, Alcatraz, the way we're right on the Hudson River in this old building. I've served more than one week already and I have less than two to go. My outside's healing faster than my inside."

"Dr. Ginario seems to have a thing for three-week recoveries," I noted.

"That's not all he has a 'thing' for," Jess said. "You know that cute nurse, Judy? Well, a guy can learn a lot from Dr. Ginario. The man is smooth."

I was getting the idea that Jess was pretty smooth himself. He was still holding my hand. I could die at a time like this, I thought, not having a phone to call Michelle and tell her about Jess. It just wasn't fair. But as Mom always says, "Everything in life is not fair, Carly." I decided I might think life was fair if I got to see more of Jess.

Chapter Four

Thanks for Understanding

On Monday of week number three I was surprised to see Jess instead of Judy deliver my mail. "I sweet-talked her out of it," he said. "You sure have a lot of admirers. Five out of ten envelopes have returns to male names."

"Let me see," I said as he waved the letters out of my reach.

"So there *is* a special someone you're hoping to hear from," he teased.

"I wish," I said.

Judy walked in, grabbed the letters from Jess, and handed them to me. "This kid has too much energy for his own good." She laughed and shook her head.

Jess looked her up and down like a cat eyeing his dinner and said, "Not bad looking."

"I am not lunch, but it seems I am your answering service," Judy said. "Your phone has been ringing off the hook. You have a phone call right now from Diana. Teresa and Laura called earlier. Also call your mother if you want her to bring your blue bathrobe." Judy shook her head as she walked out of the room.

Jess followed her. "Good job, Judy! You can be my secretary anytime."

I laughed, enjoying how good Jess made me feel. I opened my mail, listening to Jess joking with Judy. I wanted to talk like that, too, joke back and forth with guys. Five out of ten envelopes I opened were not from boys, but then Jess didn't know names such as Sam and Jeri and Andy were really Samantha, Jerice and Andrea. I wondered who Diana, Teresa, and Laura were in Jess's life. I searched the pile of letters till I found one from Michelle. She never skipped a day. I ripped open the envelope and read her latest news.

Dear Carly,

I wish you weren't so far away or at least that you had a phone. I'm so sorry you got hurt. I think about you all the time. I miss you sooooooo much. I feel so bad thinking of you alone in a hospital all the way in the country. I can't wait to see you. I'm sorry I went to the lake with you. If I weren't there, you wouldn't have gotten hurt. I wish you had gone out on a date with Eric when he asked you instead of saying, no, you were going on vacation with your parents. Then you wouldn't be hurt. School is the same...boring. Everyone asks me about you and I have to tell about the accident over and over again. It makes me sad.

Last night I washed my hair and didn't dry

it. I just left it loose and went to sleep with it all wet. You should see it this morning. Not fuzzy. Just curly.

I'm writing this letter during health. We're watching a movie for a change. It's so old, it's in black and white. If my writing is crooked, it's because the room is darkened. The shades are down. I just know one of the shades will snap up suddenly and scare me to death.

Well, I gotta go. The bell's about to ring. I'm sorry this letter isn't longer. I'm sorry about everything.

Love and XXXXX
Millions of them

Michelle

P.S. Don't forget I miss you
soooooo much.

Michelle's letter made me wish I could just wash my hair myself. Big deal if it's curly or straight. Clean would be nice. Washing it myself would be the greatest. I thought how boring school seemed until I compared it with being sick in bed for weeks.

Michelle seemed to be suffering almost as much as I was. I had less pain lately, I thought, unless like now, I moved the wrong way. The pain reminded me of the time I was measured for my brace. I thought about the man who came in with Dr. Ginario and placed brown wrapping paper under the length of my body. I thought about how he took measurements with a tape measure, then traced the outline of my body with a black pencil. I could still hear the man's words: "In a few days your brace will be ready." A few days in the hospital is like a few months anywhere else. I couldn't believe how slowly time went.

I put the get-well cards aside. When Mom came up tonight I'd ask her to tape them to the wall behind me with the others. It's great to see how many people sent cards, I thought. I really appreciated every one I received. It still surprised me, getting cards from kids who barely knew me. Then I imagined being back in school and wearing a brace. I got a sinking feeling in my stomach as I pictured my friends racing off to get the bus, or going down to someone's basement to dance—forgetting I couldn't do those things. I'd be left out of everything. Oh, they'd pity me—that would be the worst. Maybe they wouldn't want me around after a while. I fought back tears as I picked up the last unopened envelope—a note from my father. He wrote:

Dear Carly,

I'm determined to overcome this hospital phobia and make it to your bedside by the end of the week. I'm thinking of you and praying you get better. I figured if I put it in writing, like a business contract, I'd have a better chance

of accomplishing my goal. Thanks for understanding.

Love,
Dad

The problem was, I didn't really understand. Fathers weren't supposed to act this way. They were supposed to be there when you needed them. The letter depressed me. Didn't Dad care about how I was feeling? If he loved me enough, nothing should have kept him from my side—no hospital phobia or business problems or anything. I wiped away a tear that trickled down my cheek and felt very alone as Tina snored away across the room, then I heard a commotion out in the hall.

I couldn't get to my mirror fast enough to see what was going on, and the only voice loud enough to hear was the head nurse's.

"You all expect to visit?" Mrs. Todd was saying. "You're all from out of town? I don't care if you're from Europe. We have rules around here, you know. Visiting hours are not until two o'clock and you may only go in two at a time."

I wondered who had come to visit. All my friends were from out of town, but I doubted they'd be able to make the trip to see me. So at two o'clock I was really surprised when I looked up to see Michelle and another friend, Jeri, appear next to my bed. "I wish I could sit up and hug you," I said happily. "You traveled all this way just for me?"

"To the end of the earth," Michelle said.

"Move over," Jeri said. "After the train trip we could use a rest. How ya doing? Everyone's talking about you at school."

"I wish I could move over," I said. "I wish I could be in school and take rotten tests and complain about homework."

Then I looked at Michelle. She'd turned pale as a ghost and I knew she was fighting back tears. I know that feeling very well. I reached out for her hand.

"I'm okay. Really. I'm getting better every minute." I tried to reassure her.

"I cried all the way home when your neighbors drove me back to Brooklyn after your accident. You got hurt and it's all my fault. It was my side of the hammock. I shouldn't have let you switch sides. All the years since we were little kids together you always took all the risks."

"Come here," I said, patting the bed. She came closer. "It wasn't your fault. What can I do to get you to believe that?"

"I don't know," she said as she tried to hug me without touching me—kind of hovering close above me, afraid I'd break. I reached my arms up as high as I could and patted her back. A tear fell from her eyes and landed on my cheek. I willed myself not to cry. If I did, I might not stop. Besides, my parents and Michelle were upset enough without me carrying on.

"Michelle, we came to cheer Carly up, not to turn this place into *General Hospital*," Jeri said. "Carly, I have to tell you what happened at the movies Saturday."

"What?" I asked.

"Picture this," she said. "Seven girls and Freddy."

"I can imagine," I said, and laughed.

Laughing together was good in a way, and yet in another way it made me feel sadder and even more left out. Feelings are so confusing.

"I better let someone else in," Jeri said. "Michelle gets to stay. She's driven us crazy for days wanting to see you. 'Bye, kiddo," she said, and kissed my cheek.

"Thanks for coming all this way," I called as she left. "My father can't even make it into my room from the hall. I don't want to feel angry with him," I said to Michelle. "But I do."

Michelle took the moment alone to blow her nose and say, "You mean your father doesn't visit you? I'd be angry if it were my father!" Her words comforted me. "Do you have a lot of pain?"

"Not really," I said, not wanting to upset her more. "Just now and then."

"Oh. . . . I spoke to all your teachers. They basically said to tell you not to worry about the work—to just get better. . . except Mme. Larson. She gave me this French storybook and said to tell you to read and translate the condensed version of *Les Misérables* and return to class prepared to give a speech about Jean Valjean's innocence."

"Terrific," I said. "What a kind human being she is. Now I have something else to worry about."

"Just ignore her. What can she do? You have a good excuse, thanks to me."

Before I could respond to that remark, two more friends were beside me. Andrea and Freddy.

"I snuck in," Freddy said. "I wore these white pants and shirt and I walked in with Andrea as if I worked here."

"They probably thought you were a young-looking male nurse," I said.

Freddy took my hand. "Let me check your pulse."

My pulse didn't race like it did when Jess touched me.

"Freddy and I are going together," Andrea said. "We finally got past being just friends."

"That's great," I said. "Good luck, you guys." What I really felt like saying was, oh, no, everyone's having a terrific time while I'm cooped up in a hospital bored to death.

I heard arguing in the hall, followed by Mrs. Todd's announcing loudly, "This is a hospital, not a school dormitory," ending with a shush that if written in a book would take up an entire page. At the same time two more friends snuck into my room giggling.

"That's Samantha and Donna out there pretending to be arguing to cause a distraction. It worked, too," Andrea said.

I looked around and counted. "I haven't laughed like this in weeks. Actually, I couldn't have laughed like this a week ago." I felt a glimmer of hope. I must be getting better. Maybe I wouldn't need an operation. I felt so good until I laughed too hard and got a fierce shooting pain that stopped all our giggles and turned Michelle pale again.

"Oh, no," she said. "Did you hurt yourself? I arranged this whole group visit. Maybe it was too much for you? Maybe I shouldn't have done it?"

I had to wait to catch my breath before I could calm her. "I'm all right," I said, but I don't think she believed me. Freddy and Andrea said good-bye, and Michelle said she'd better go and let the last two kids come in.

"I've been working on our list of most romantic couples," I said to cheer her up. "Write these down. If we use real-life people, I think we could include my doctor and nurse, Dr. Ginario and Judy."

"If we add from real life, how about Freddy and Andrea? They're a real item at school," Michelle said. "Freddy actually carried Andrea across a big puddle yesterday when it stormed. I was dying to call and tell you right away."

"It's strange to be the last person to know what's going on in your own group," I said. "Keep writing, anyway."

"Every day, I promise. By the way, that guy you turned down keeps asking about you."

"He does? Very interesting. Keep me informed."

"I will," she said as she left.

The kids who visited me last barely got to say hello and good-bye before Mrs. Todd ended my visiting hours early. I was mad. I wished I could walk right out of here with them. "Will I ever walk again?" I silently asked God. "Please let me walk out of here," I begged. "Please let the brace not be too ugly. What'll I do if I can't dance again or swim or . . . okay, I'll deal with it if I can't dance. But I have to walk. Please."

I was deep in thought so I was totally surprised when I turned my head and saw Eric, the boy whose

35

invitation I'd turned down just three weeks ago. He seemed to appear from out of nowhere.

"Eric!"

"Hi, Carly. How are ya doing?"

"Okay, I guess."

"This must be tough on you," he said.

"Yeah, it's no picnic. But I love seeing you. I've had a lot of visitors, but you're the best one." I rambled nervously. Eric didn't say anything. Why did I bring up love? I asked myself. What will he think with me talking to him about love. And I never say "it's no picnic." Tina says that.

Eric changed the subject. "Michelle told me she and some kids would be visiting you today. I had to work at my father's pharmacy." He shifted his weight from one foot to the other. "I kept thinking about you. So I took the next train up." He seemed out of breath. Maybe he was nervous. I felt a little breathless, too, and I certainly hadn't walked or run anywhere.

"Oh, here," Eric said, "I almost forgot. I brought you some flowers."

"Thanks. They're beautiful." We talked some more. I wonder why I didn't notice the time while Eric was standing at my side.

Chapter Five

He's Nice.
But He's Not for You

Why did Mrs. Todd have to send Eric home after only a short visit? He'd come so far. Just when we were getting to know each other. I almost wished all the other kids hadn't stayed so long. Doesn't anyone understand this is still my life even if I am flat on my back in bed? But what could I do but get angry? I was so angry. Calm down, I told myself, or you'll blow up. I battled myself to be in control.

I concentrated on how Eric had looked at me with— it seemed as if his brown eyes were feeling my pain more than I was. I closed my eyes and pictured our fingers brushing as he handed me the flowers.

Now as I held the flowers, I was glad I had proof that Eric had actually visited. I could still hear his words in my mind: "I'm glad I could see you, even if it's just for a few minutes. I tend to picture things worse than they are. Maybe we can go out when you get back to school?"

"Maybe," I'd answered him, thinking he might not want to go out with a girl wearing a brace.

"Hey, Carly. You definitely get the Miss Popularity award for today," Jess said.

"Friends!" I said smiling. "Come in. I love having visitors."

"You too tired?" Jess asked.

"Talking sounds good."

"Where's Tina?" Jess asked.

"Leo said he was taking her to the waiting room to romance her. They're such a cute couple."

"Yeah. So, was that your boyfriend who just left?" he asked.

"He was definitely a boy and he was definitely a friend."

"You're not giving away much information," he teased.

"Look who's talking. I saw you walking three girls to the elevator, and you haven't said anything about them."

"What do you want to know?"

"Everything!"

"One of them is about your age," Jess said, "and I'm madly in love with her and have been for years."

"Were the other two your sisters?"

"I like to be mysterious. Give you something to think about." Jess leaned close to me as he spoke. "So how'd it go with your friends? They cheer you up?"

"I guess. Sometimes I felt like I cheered them up. My friend Michelle, she feels so guilty about my accident."

"The kid in the hammock with you?"

"Yes."

"Well, she should be cheering you up, not the other way around," Jess said.

"I worry about her," I said.

"Worry about keeping your toes wiggling."

"I do. But you don't know Michelle. She's the best friend anyone could have. Maybe you never had a friend like that?"

"I guess you're right," Jess said. "It's great that you're so understanding. I'd just worry about myself."

"I guess we're different," I said. "But I like you anyway!"

He got up to go and took my hand in his. "You've got good friends. You have a good family. You're lucky. It's really great when people come through for you."

"Sure," I said, and swallowed the lump in my throat as I thought of my father.

"Hang in there," Jess said, and he went back down the hall as Judy walked into the room. "Dr. Ginario will be here any minute with the technician."

I hoped I wouldn't scream when I saw the monstrosity. On the other hand, if I wore the brace, I could be sitting up on my bed with my legs dangling over the side when Mom and Dad got here later. Maybe *then* Dad would do more than wave and say hi from the doorway and disappear. He'd accomplished that much, but why couldn't he take two steps farther and be in the room? Then I could really see him and we could talk and he could kiss my forehead like he always used to. I thought about yesterday when I saw him in my mirror. He looked awful, pale and jittery. Only now did I realize how disappointed I was in him. Disappointed in my own father. That was an all-time first.

I must have been soothing myself while I waited for Dr. Ginario and the brace person, because I suddenly realized I was humming the chorus to the lullaby "Rock-a-Bye Baby." But the last stanza sent a chill through me. "When the bough breaks, the cradle will fall, and down will come baby—cradle and all." Just like a hammock, I thought.

Then Jess walked back into my room crutchless and said, "I've been sprung. Ginario just said I can go home tomorrow." He looked as if he were about to leap in the air.

"That's great, Jess!" I lied. How could I feel happy for him when it meant he wouldn't be around anymore to flirt with, or to make me laugh and feel good? He'd probably want to forget all about this hospital and everyone in it.

"He loves me; he loves me not?" Jess pointed to the wilting daisies I still clutched in my hands. "What's the matter, Miss America, too many guys to choose from? You had quite a crowd in here." He leaned over and kissed me quickly on the lips as if it were the most natural thing in the world. Then he laughed and limped out as Dr. Ginario entered with Judy at his side and the brace person behind him. I could still feel Jess's lips on mine. I wondered if I was blushing.

Tina came racing in as if a major event were about to take place. "Hurray, you're getting your brace!" Tina reminded me of a cheerleader rallying the team spirit. I was glad she was here with me. I couldn't imagine being in the hospital without her, especially since Jess was leaving. Tina understands me so well, sometimes I think she has ESP.

"Here you are." The brace man unwrapped the brown paper and held up what looked like a corset or a girdle my great-grandmother might have worn, only it had big wires covered with flesh-colored material that slipped over my shoulders.

"You won't see the brace when you wear clothing over it," Dr. Ginario added. "And we used a light-weight foundation product so it doesn't weigh a ton."

I closed my eyes. When I open them the brace will look like a beautiful lacy strapless bra, I told myself, working hard to stifle the major scream building inside me. But I started to panic. I won't feel like me in that thing. I'm a mover, a doer. I have to be free. I have to be free. I shouted the words inwardly. Then, taking a deep breath, I opened my eyes. The brace was still there, looking even uglier than before.

"You'll have an hourglass figure," Tina said gaily. "Like in olden days. It'll push your bosom up and you'll look great."

I was embarrassed, but everyone else laughed.

"Where's your sense of humor, Carly?" Judy asked. "You can't misplace it now when you need it most. Think of the brace as a fashion statement. You'll start a new trend." Judy took my hand in hers and gave it a squeeze.

I didn't say a word.

"Out, everyone," Judy said. "Give Carly some privacy while I show her how to put on this elegant undergarment."

"Judy can make anyone feel better about anything," Dr. Ginario said, and put his hand on her shoulder. Dr. Ginario couldn't see it, but Judy glowed at his words. Observing her took my mind off the brace. As Judy closed the curtain around the two of us, I thought, yes, Dr. Ginario and Judy should definitely be added to the most-romantic-couples list. I'd have to tell Michelle.

Judy rolled me onto my side and placed the brace on the bed. Then she rolled me back onto it. She helped me slip my arms into the openings and fastened the straps of the brace tightly across my stomach.

"Too tight," I gasped.

"So you *can* talk," she said, and loosened and refastened the Velcro straps, which made a ripping sound. "Just checking. Now that you've found your tongue, what do you think of all this?"

"I think I know what a hot dog feels like inside those tight plastic wrappers," I said.

Judy laughed. She stood back and surveyed me, like a pushy saleswoman in a dress shop. "This is you. This is definitely you. Now don't go anywhere. I want to get your robe." Judy opened the curtain, baring me to the world in my new brace.

The joking had helped me hold back my feelings about the brace, but finally I had to get the words out. "I can't breathe in this ugly thing! How will I change for gym? Everyone in the locker room will suddenly be quiet and stare at me. Stupid rule. You have to change into gym clothes even if you're excused from taking gym."

No one said anything.

I ran my fingers over the brace from top to bottom and side to side. For a moment I thought I might cry, but then I remembered that now I could wear a robe and sit up for the first time in weeks.

The brace man checked the fit. Then after he okayed it and left, Judy put my bathrobe on me and moved back to let Dr. Ginario get close to the bed.

"I'm going to help you sit up," Dr. Ginario said. "We'll take it nice and slowly because you'll probably feel dizzy at first."

As Dr. Ginario put his hands under each of my arms and gently eased me forward, I looked straight into his eyes, noticing how strong and handsome he was. I was determined to be brave and ignore the scary weak feeling in the pit of my stomach, until the entire room started swirling around in front of me and my stomach did a flip.

"How are you doing?" Tina asked.

"I feel sick," I mumbled.

"When you're sitting up, I can give you a peppermint to suck on. It'll settle your stomach."

"Close your eyes, then open them slowly," Dr. Ginario said as he and Judy turned me so my legs dangled over the side of the bed.

As I opened my eyes, the spinning gradually stopped. It occurred to me that even if I could stand without falling on my face, I'd forgotten how to walk. I looked down at my legs. They looked skinnier.

Then I stared out the window. The sun was shining and sparkling on the Hudson River below. It looked beautiful.

"I'll go get Jess and we'll have a little party," Tina said. "It's important to celebrate each step forward. It helps you get better."

"How did you get so smart?" I asked Tina.

"Talk shows," she said, and left.

"Can I surprise my parents and sit like this when they come to visit tonight?" I asked.

"Absolutely," Dr. Ginario answered. "Any other questions?"

"Yes. One more. When can I walk to the bathroom?"

"Tomorrow Judy will take you for your first walk. You have to take this literally step by step. Nice and slow. You're not ready for any marathons, but I think you may be able to make it to the john. I like a patient with high hopes," he joked.

Tina came back and announced with a wave, "And heeeere's Carly!"

Jess appeared and shouted, "Hurray!"

I was sitting up, big deal, but I felt as if I'd just won a race or something.

"So Jess and Tina go home tomorrow," Judy said too cheerfully.

"And Carly may get to go home by the end of this week if all goes well," Dr. Ginario said.

The words "if all goes well" made my heart sink. It took a minute for his other words to hit me.

"Tina, you're going home tomorrow, too?" I asked,

not wanting to think about myself. "You didn't tell me."

"I was planning on telling you later. I didn't want to spoil your good news. You'll see. You'll be so busy walking around, you'll forget all about us. People come and go in hospitals, Carly. That's life."

I wanted to say, "Don't go, Tina. Don't leave me here alone. I'm frightened. You're the only one who notices how I feel. I need you to tell me everything is okay." But I didn't. I didn't want to cry. All I said was "Why?" And then I just got very quiet.

"Maybe it's because when you're well you want to forget when you weren't—and everyone who reminds you of that time. You're young yet, sweetie," Tina said. "You're just finding out there are different kinds of friendships."

Dinner was being served, or rather rolled noisily, into each room. Tonight I could sit up and eat. "This feels great," I said to Jess and Tina, who ate dinner with me to celebrate. "Even the unidentifiable object masquerading as meat tastes good." I can sit up! Hurray for me! I said to myself.

The best part of the day was the moment when Mom and Dad came to the doorway and saw me sitting up, with my legs dangling, wearing my pretty pastel-striped robe. Their eyes glistened with happy surprise. "You're sitting up!" Mom shouted. "How wonderful!" Dad was almost at my side. I could almost touch him when he turned pale and started to sweat and wipe his brow.

"It's okay, Dad," I said, "I'm getting better. Everything will be all right." I reached my hand out to him expecting him to take it and hug me, maybe even cry with joy.

Instead he disappointed me again, even on my special day. "I'm sorry, Carly. I just can't stay. Forgive me." He turned and raced out the door just as Leo, Tina's husband, came in.

"Way to go, Carly!" Leo said.

I was so embarrassed. Jess and Tina and her husband had seen my father walk out on me. How could he let me down like that in front of my friends? Forgive him? I couldn't forgive him.

Jess tried to cheer me up. "Em-brace me, my sweet, em-brace-able you," he sang, emphasizing the word *brace*. "I'll be back later," he added. I got sad thinking about all the good-byes I'd have to handle tomorrow.

After Jess left, Mom tried to cheer me up. "I'm sorry, honey. Your father's been trying very hard. These things take time. We've all been under a lot of stress." She took my hand in hers.

I fought back tears. "You mean the stress about business? Do you have to find a new store to move to?"

"Yes. That's part of it," she answered. "And it's not..." She stopped in midsentence.

"You mean, Pam's marriage problems?" I asked. I wanted to know what was going on in my own family.

"You just get better. I don't want you worrying, too."

"Ma, I may be in the hospital, but I'm still part of the

family. Stop sparing me and tell me the truth. I ought to know what's happening to my own sister."

"There may be a divorce. We're not sure yet. I don't think she's sure yet."

"A divorce!" I said. "I don't believe it."

"Never a dull moment," Mom said. "But let's talk about happier things. Okay? I don't feel like talking about our troubles."

Once again my mother didn't want me to express my feelings. I wished I could talk to Pam. Get-well cards with scribbled messages on them just made me miss her more. Why did she have to live all the way in Chicago? And a divorce was about as unromantic a thought as could be, but I couldn't talk to Mom about it now.

Instead, I told Mom about my friends' visiting and Michelle's guilty feelings.

"She'll get over it," Mom said, and then changed the subject. "Tell me about Jess. He's certainly good-looking. Does he go to school or work? What kind of person is he?" She asked me seven hundred questions about him.

"I can't answer all your questions," I said. "I just know he's very nice and I'm sad that he's leaving."

She ended our visit with the same words I remembered her telling my sister before she got engaged. "He's nice—but he's not for you. This Jess person."

She makes up her mind about people on sight, I thought. Just because she was right about my brother-in-law doesn't mean she's right about Jess.

I decided to change the subject. "When I go home

next week, what's Daddy going to do? Maybe it's not the hospital, maybe it's my being injured that makes him anxious."

That would be some homecoming, a father who was uncomfortable around his invalid daughter, a friend weighted down with guilt, business problems, my sister's possible divorce, and—oh, yes—the presentation, in French no less, of Jean Valjean's innocence. Me, in the hideous brace, in front of the whole class, making a speech. Once word got out about my brace it would probably scare off Eric and any other romantic possibilities. I suddenly needed more than another peppermint. I didn't know what to worry about first, second, third, or fourth.

Chapter Six

We'll Be There
When We Get There

Late at night Jess snuck past the nurses' station and
joined me and Tina for a good-bye party. We talked
and joked and had a great time. After Tina fell asleep, I
asked Jess the questions Mom had asked me about
him.

"I'm surviving high school by the skin of my teeth,"
he said. "I work part-time not far from here rebuilding
engines. After I graduate I want to save up enough
money to own my own business someday, get married,
have half a dozen kids and a Kawasaki motorcycle."

"What kind of business?" I asked.

"I'm not sure," he said. "I just like the word
'entrepreneur.' When I found out it meant a person
who starts his own business, I knew that's what I
wanted to be." When he said the word "entrepreneur,"
it rolled off his tongue like a melody.

"Your turn," he said. "Spill it. I want to hear about
you."

I told him how worried I was about my scary French
project and how much I missed my best friend, Michelle.

I didn't tell him about Eric in particular. I just explained, "I'm nervous about what the kids at school are going to think about my brace. I'm afraid they'll treat me differently. Leave me out of things, maybe." It felt good to talk about it.

"Don't let them," he said. "Just remember, Carly, you're a winner. They better not mess with you."

"One last thing," I said as Jess got up to leave. "Can you tell me some more about the girl I remind you of? The one you, uh, said you loved all your life."

"You mean the gorgeous one with the big blue eyes? The heartbreaker, we call her."

"I guess," I said.

"You'd love her. Just like you, the most important thing in her life is the telephone. And she fusses at her hair like you do when you think I'm not looking."

My cheeks turned red at his words. "So who is she? Your girlfriend?" I asked, getting the subject off me.

"Nah. I got a million girlfriends, but she's special. She's my favorite sister. Maybe because she's the baby of the family and the other two are older than me . . . and bossy."

Great, I thought later as I tried to fall asleep. I remind him of his baby sister. How romantic. And he'd reminded me of a time when telephones and hair were my biggest worries and got me seriously crazy. Now I had so many real worries. How could I have thought those other things were so important?

The next morning was awful. I'd known Tina for only a little over two weeks, but it was so hard to say good-bye. I tried to be happy for her and Jess—after all, they were going home...and I know that's the goal in a hospital. But I was sad for me. I watched Tina pack up her get-well cards, robe and slippers, the stuffed dog Leo had given her, and the photo of Leo, so kind-looking.

Jess came into the room and said good-bye with a kiss for Tina and me, gave us a thumbs-up sign and a parting, "Knock 'em dead, you two."

I handed him a paper with my Brooklyn phone number and address and my summer phone number at the lake. He took it politely. I thought he'd give me his, but he didn't.

He put the slip of paper in the back pocket of his jeans and walked out. I pictured it in shreds weeks later after going through the laundry, both it and me forgotten. Would I ever see him again? Would I ever forget him?

In my hand mirror I saw a pretty girl waiting in the hall. I saw Jess kiss her before she wheeled him onto the elevator. She looked about eighteen, the same age he was. He never mentioned a special girlfriend and I never saw her visiting.

Next, Tina said good-bye. She hugged me.

"Because of the brace, I only feel where your arms touch my arms. I can't even feel a hug," I said. "I think I'll hate that most of all. I love being hugged."

"But you can still hug back," Tina said. "Don't you forget that. Anyway, you'll see, in life the giving's better than the getting." She took the slip of paper with my address and gave me one with hers. "If I don't hear from you, I'll figure you're doing fine," she said. "Remember what I said about hospital friends. You get very close very fast, and very distant as soon as you go home. Not like your friend Michelle, or that boy Eric who traveled all this way to see you."

Was that her way of telling me to forget about Jess?

I was alone in the empty room. I felt empty inside, too. "Tina, how could you leave me now when I need you? Who will cheer me on when I get to walk—if I can walk?" No one was around to hear my words or to see my tears. The tissue box was out of reach. I didn't even care. I just sniffed. I didn't eat lunch. Even if it had been the best hamburger and milk shake in the world, I couldn't have eaten a bite.

In the afternoon, Judy showed me how to put my brace on myself. I rolled onto it and strapped myself in before I sat up. My arms weren't strong enough yet to push myself up, so she helped me. I stood up and took a few steps to a chair near the window. I stared at the river. It went on and on. "Just like life," I could hear Tina saying.

I felt like sobbing but I controlled myself. When would Dr. Ginario say I could walk, I wondered? My imagination took over. What if I couldn't walk? What if my skinny legs could no longer hold up my body and I collapsed like a Halloween skeleton decoration? What if I had to use a bedpan for the rest of my life? There was no Tina today to see me turn pale with terror and help me. I cried and cried.

The next day, I got to walk to the bathroom. My legs, skinny as they were, still held me up, wobbly at first, but they still knew what to do.

"Don't let go of me, Judy," I said.

"Don't worry. I've got you," she answered.

Then I started to laugh. "Okay. Let go of me." I took the last three steps into the bathroom on my own, reaching for the sink to steady myself.

"Well done!" she said.

I laughed till I had to get on the seat real fast. The flushing was an important moment. Judy waited outside the door and laughed at my excitement. I wished Tina were there to say something funny. I felt as if I'd hit my first home run and no one was looking.

Finally the day came when I could take a real walk. First I walked to the phone and called Michelle, even though I knew she was in school. It just felt good to dial her number and leave a message on her answering machine. I enjoyed imagining how happy she'd be when she got home, played back her messages, and heard my voice. All I said was our usual, "Hi, it's me. What do you want to do next weekend?"

I walked back to my room. I was exhausted; me, the same person who on field day wins at least one race. Forget about field day this year.

But the best part of walking was surprising my parents by waiting for them at the elevator. I never actually saw a smile grow on a person before. We laughed, and I thought I felt their hugs right through my brace, even though I knew that wasn't possible.

We walked up and down the hall. "Be careful, these waxed floors can be slippery," Mom said.

"Slow down. There's no fire. Nice and easy. That's the way," Dad added.

"Poor baby," Mom said, pitying me of all things. Tina would never have pitied me.

My father changed the subject. "This is as exciting as when you took your first steps."

"You never walked. You ran. You just got up and ran as if you'd been walking all your life," Mom added, and I felt a wave of sadness.

As long as we stayed in the hallway, Dad was all right. But when I was tired and wanted to go back to bed, he said, "I feel like such a baby. I've just got to get out of here. I'm sorry to be such a disappointment to you, Carly. I never should have given you that hammock." And he left before I could say another word.

He sounded as guilty as Michelle, I thought. Why did they insist on taking the blame for my accident? *I'd* tied the stupid knot that hadn't held, and no one else had anything to do with it. Didn't Dad even remember how happy I'd been when he surprised me with that hammock? "It was a gift from a sea captain customer who couldn't pay his clothing bill," he'd said. "It's from the Philippines." I remembered relaxing and dreaming in it.

Finally it was my turn to leave, to say good-byes, to pack up my cards and letters and slippers and robe. "You can take the plastic water pitcher and cup, it's yours," the white-haired nurse said.

"Thanks, but no thanks," I answered. "I don't ever want to see those things again."

Would I feel that way about Tina and Jess, too? Or would they feel that way about me? I thought about what Tina had said about hospital friends and wanting to forget unhappy memories.

Dr. Ginario signed my discharge papers. "In four weeks set up an appointment to see me again. You'll have to stop by the hospital first for X rays, and then I'll be able to tell if you're growing straight or if your spine is curving and needs correction."

"Okay," I said. I guess he didn't want to spoil my day by mentioning the word "surgery." But I knew what he meant. I just wouldn't think about it. I'd bury the thought.

"And remember," he said, "you can do things in moderation. Just save the first dance for me. Deal?"

"Deal," I said. Then Judy came in and I added, "But I bet you'd rather dance every dance with Judy. Right?"

"Not a bad idea," he said, and Judy's eyes sparkled.

Judy walked me to the elevator, hugged me, and as she walked away, said, "I'll miss you."

"Thanks for everything, Judy," I called. "I don't know what I would have done without you."

Mom pushed my wheelchair to the car, and Dad helped me in. He and Mom had lined the backseat with pillows. They handled me as if I were made out of glass.

Why this sudden wave of sadness? I wondered. For weeks I had dreamed of going home. But now I felt apprehensive. Everything would be different. Everyone would treat me differently. I pictured it all in my head. First they'd be real sweet. They'd do anything for me, because they'd feel sorry for me. Then everyone would get tired of opening doors for me and

55

getting this or that. They'd be glad when I wasn't around.

Fortunately, at this point my stomach growled insistently and gave me something else to think about.

"I'm starved," I announced.

"Let's stop at the coffee shop down the block," Dad suggested. "I've spent many visiting hours waiting there." We could have walked to it, but he insisted on driving.

We sat at the counter.

"A hamburger with ketchup and onions, french fries, and a chocolate milk shake, please." I ordered the meal I'd been thinking about for weeks.

I was surprised when the counterman and the waitress said excitedly, "You must be Carly."

"How do you know my name?" I asked. "I've never been in here before."

"We've been rooting for you," the waitress explained.

"I feel as if I know you, Carly," the counterman added. "We started to call seven to eight P.M. 'the Carly hour,' because that was the time your dad would come in here for a bite to eat, and all he could ever talk about was you. We've heard all about your recovery."

It was almost like a party as we all ate and when Dad asked for the check, the man said, "It's on the house."

"There really are some nice people in this world," Dad said, and Mom and I agreed.

The ride back home seemed endless. Even with the pillows protecting me from the car's jolts and bumps on the road, my back still ached.

"Stretch out so you're comfortable," Mom insisted.

I wiggled into the best position I could. After a few minutes of driving, I asked, "Are we there yet?"

And I felt as if things were getting back to normal when Mom answered, "We'll be there when we get there."

MAY

Chapter Seven

I've Only
Got Two Hands

My father had barely turned the car into our drive-way when Michelle came bounding out of her house next door. She must have been watching for us at the window.

Michelle hugged me. When her hands touched the hardware of the brace I wore under my blouse and jeans, I felt her pull back as if a sudden heat had burnt her fingers. Was she afraid? My best friend afraid of me? The thought hurt more than my back. I felt sad. What was it Tina said to do? Her words came back to me: "Just hug first." I reached out and hugged Michelle until she relaxed.

"It's late, but Michelle can come in for a little while," Mom said. "But you have to lie down and rest, be-cause you've had a long, tiring day."

Michelle walked with me to my room. "I am so happy to see my bedroom," I said. I touched my desk and rocking chair, admiring their familiar pink color.

"My own room!" I shouted out loud. "You can't imagine how good it feels to be home." I looked in my mirror. I could see the bump of the brace bulging at my shoulders. I turned away. "My own bed!" I said lying down. "It's the best bed in the world!"

Michelle sat down cross-legged at the foot of it. She sat very still, as if afraid to shake the bed in any way.

"I'm okay, Michelle. Relax, I won't break."

"I just feel so bad for you," she said.

"I'm doing fine." I reached for her hand. "Did you hear? My father spoke to the principal and I'm going to get an elevator pass. I don't have to walk the stairs at school for the rest of the term. And you know I'll need someone to carry my books, so I'll be getting an elevator pass for two."

"All the injured football players ride the elevator." Michelle smiled, catching on.

"I know. Want to be my official book carrier?" I asked. "You never can tell who you'll meet on the elevator."

We both laughed.

"You could drop one of my books and maybe some hunk with his ankle in a cast will pick it up for you. That would be romantic," I said. Before too long we were talking about romance, our favorite subject. It felt good not to think about anything else. Almost like old times.

"The elevator could be jam-packed and some gorgeous guy would be crushed up against you," Michelle suggested. "Maybe Eric would carry your books for you one day. He asked me when you were coming home from the hospital."

"He did? Did he say he'd call me?"

"He didn't say," she said.

His interest in me would probably evaporate once he saw the stiff way I walked and the humps the brace made on top of my shoulders. He'd be polite and quietly disappear from my life, just the way Jess and Tina would, too. I thought about Eric's visit to the hospital and the daisies he'd brought me. What would I say to him when we met again?

"You're quiet all of a sudden. What's wrong?" Michelle asked.

"I don't know. Worrying about things, I guess."

"Like what?"

"Like can I walk all day without falling on my face?—pretty unromantic. I wish I could be the same old me—when romance was the most important thing I worried about."

Michelle was getting upset again, so I changed the subject. I told her about Jess and Tina, and what Tina had said about never seeing hospital friends again.

"But we'll always be friends, even when we're grandmothers," Michelle said, and reached for my hand. We laughed.

"It's funny to think of us growing old together," I said.

"Yeah." Michelle glanced at my clock radio and squealed, "Ten forty-five! I better get going." She reached for my phone, like she's done a million other times, and called home. "I'm leaving Carly's," she said, and hung up. "My father will be halfway here before I'm even out the door. I'm still treated like I'm two years old."

"Parents!" I sighed.

Just after Michelle left, the phone rang. I couldn't maneuver myself fast enough to get it on the first ring. I'd have to practice. I wondered who was calling so late. I also wondered if my parents forgot about me. Maybe they were used to not having me around. "Mom!" I called. No answer. "Dad?" I tried again with the same result.

I got up and walked down the hall to my parents' bedroom. "Calm down," I heard my father say. I wondered if he was having more business problems. "Take it easy. Don't do anything you may regret later," he added.

"What is she going to do?" I heard my mother say to my father. "Does she sound very upset? Maybe we should fly out there. But then what would we do about Carly?"

This was definitely not about their store. It must be Pam and her marital problems. I remembered Mom's talking about it in the hospital. She let me know that Pam sent her love and best wishes but was too busy and upset to write long letters. It's funny how solutions to everyone else's problems always seem simple. I wondered why my parents didn't offer to fly her here from Chicago. They must have read my mind because the next thing Dad said was, "I'm sending you a plane ticket. Maybe you just need some time away."

I didn't mean to eavesdrop. I continued into my parents' room just as they were saying good-bye. At the sight of me Dad said, "Hold on a minute, Pam, your sister wants to say hello."

He put the phone in my hand.

"Hi, Pam. . . . Yeah. It's great to be home. . . . Nah. It doesn't hurt too much. Just when I'm tired or the weather's going to change or I bend the wrong way. . . . That's okay. I know you were thinking of me—the cards were cute. So what's up with you and the perfect catch? Sounds like you want to throw him back." At least I made her laugh. My parents didn't even crack a smile. I thought about Warren the orthodontist. Handsome, charming, and potentially rich, if you look at the wired teeth around any junior high school. Who would have guessed that he would turn out to be such a jerk? Pam said something that made me laugh, and then we said good-bye. After I hung up, I repeated it to my parents. "Pam's thinking of wiring Warren's mouth shut if he doesn't stop putting her down in front of their friends." What had happened to the guy who always greeted Pam with a kiss and a single long-stemmed rose?

I decided Michelle and I had some more to figure out about romance. Were Judy and Dr. Ginario a romantic couple because they weren't married? Come to think of it, the last present I remember my father giving my mother was a microwave. Real romantic.

"You need some help getting ready for bed?" Mom asked. "We'll have to figure out how to give you a sponge bath without waterlogging your sheets and mattress."

"Good point," I said. "How about putting a plastic tablecloth under me?"

"That should work," she agreed, and went to round

up the equipment. A simple bath for me was now a major project.

My father was on the phone with the airlines. His voice got louder and louder. "There must be a ticket from O'Hare Airport to Kennedy!" Dad's face was turning red with anger. I reached over to pat his hand, but he waved me off with an irritated gesture.

"Sorreee," I apologized sarcastically, and walked out of the room.

In my bedroom, my mother had her sleeves rolled up and a pan of water and a washcloth at her elbow.

"Mom, you are not going to give me a bath," I said. "I'm not that helpless."

"It wouldn't be the first time I bathed you," Mom reminded me.

"Ma, the last time you did that I was a baby and I had a duck in the tub. Forget it. Just help me get the brace off and out of the way. I'll lay out my pajamas and some powder and a towel. And I'll call you when I need you to be a magician and pull the tablecloth out from under me so I can dry off."

"You sure you can manage?" Mom asked. "Really, I don't mind helping you. Asking for help is nothing to be ashamed of, you know. You've only got two hands. You can't do everything yourself."

"I know. I've asked for help a lot these past few weeks. But now I have to ask you for a different kind of help."

"Sure," Mom said, and stroked my forehead.

"Help me become self-sufficient again, okay?"

"Okay," she said. "I just wish I could wave a wand

and make you better. I'd also use it to make Pam and Warren live happily ever after, and make your father relax." I pulled her head close to me and kissed her forehead.

Mom got me set up and was about to walk out of the room when my father called, "I'm going for a walk. I need to get rid of this tension. There doesn't seem to be a minute's peace anymore."

"Sorry I can't go with you tonight, honey," Mom called back. "I'm helping Carly." The door slammed before she finished her sentence. She turned to me. "I just don't know what to do to help him. He's making himself sick with worry, what with the business and Pam and your back. Not that it's your fault," she added hastily.

But I somehow felt it was my fault, and that made me angry. Didn't anyone realize what I was going through? I needed support and understanding, not guilt. But I kept my feelings to myself. Mom was worried enough already.

After my bath I felt better, so comfortable, clean, and powdered. Fresh sheets on my own bed, I thought. The best and softest place in the world. I wouldn't think about my parents or sister or even about going back to school. Not tonight. Tonight was the night I'd dreamed of for weeks, and in spite of everyone, I was going to enjoy it. At last, I was home.

Chapter Eight

What Are Friends For?

I felt funny having my parents drive me and Michelle to school my first day back. They didn't think I should ride the bus and get jostled around. The usual crowd of kids was standing out front waiting for the bell. I felt as if all eyes were staring at me when I got out of the car. My legs felt wobbly again. I hoped it was only nerves.

"Oh, it's so good to see you," Samantha squealed, racing over to me.

"Does it hurt?" Andrea whispered. But no one touched me. I felt like a science experiment where magnets repel each other when the two souths or two norths get close. I found myself looking around the crowd for Eric, but if he was there, I didn't see him, or maybe he saw me and didn't want to be seen.

"You look great," Michelle reassured me. "You can't even tell you're wearing a brace. Relax."

"Michelle, you're a lousy judge of things like that," I said. "We both know you're incredibly nearsighted. You don't even have your glasses on!" We both laughed.

Michelle carried my books. It was fun going up in

the elevator. The four flights of stairs to my homeroom would have been an effort. Michelle couldn't take her eyes off this football player with a knee injury. She almost fainted when he spoke to her.

"Excuse me," he said as he tried to get past her. She was blocking the door. After he hobbled out, we glanced at each other, acknowledging his good looks.

As we walked to class, she said, "Could I carry your books for you tomorrow, too? I've never stood that close to Harris Walsh before. I must say, I like it."

"What are friends for?" We parted at my homeroom door.

"I'll meet you back here at the bell," she said.

"Great."

By third period I was dragging myself around. What used to be such a normal pace felt hectic and tiring.

I wondered if Eric was absent. Usually I see him in the cafeteria at lunchtime. Sometimes we've stood together on the ice cream line. He always orders a vanilla pop covered with chocolate, same as I do.

Today, as Michelle and I sat down at our usual table with Sam and Andy, I noticed myself looking around the big room more than usual. I kept hoping Eric would appear, but he didn't. Freddy did, though. It was a new sight to see him squeeze in next to Andrea. They held hands and ate their sandwiches while staring into each other's eyes. "Too much romance for me," Michelle whispered, and I knew exactly what she meant.

Finally, just when I'd taken a big mouthful of my chicken salad sandwich so that I looked like a chipmunk eating nuts, Eric appeared. I breathed a sigh of relief and wondered why I'd done that. When had Eric become important to me?

The chattering voices and banging trays made his soft voice hard to hear, but I figured out what he said when he offered me a chocolate-covered ice cream pop. "So you won't have to stand on line. It's good to see you back at school, Carly. How do you feel?"

Freddy reached over and squeezed my arm. "She feels pretty good to me," he joked, and Andrea smacked his shoulder.

I wished Freddy would get up so there'd be a space for Eric to sit down, but Freddy and Andrea appeared to be glued together at the hip.

Just then a guy I knew from French class came charging up behind me. He greeted me with a smack on the shoulder and a loud, "Hey, Carly, you're back. What are you wearing under your blouse? Armor?"

I could feel my face turning red with embarrassment. And in front of Eric, too! Was it just a coincidence that Eric chose this moment to say, "Enjoy your ice cream. See ya 'round," and walked away? I wanted to crawl under my seat and disappear. Except I couldn't crawl—I couldn't even bend.

To make matters worse, my next class was French. Mme. Larson, unlike my other teachers, did not welcome me back to class. She just went right into vocabulary drill, pointing to about twenty-five French words on the blackboard that I had never seen before. At least, I thought, I'll be exempt from the French final because I got an eighty-six on the midterm. At the beginning of the semester she'd told the class her exemption policy. We thought she would be a great teacher. Were we ever wrong!

How would I get through this day? I felt exhausted already. In the hospital I would be napping now. Tina and Jess, wherever they are, probably feel tired, too. Thinking of them soothed me.

Mme. Larson's voice startled me back to the present. *"Mademoiselle?"* she said, and opened her eyes wide as if she was expecting an answer from me.

The problem was, I didn't know the question. The entire class, perfectly quiet, looked at me. I tensed up. The boy behind me knocked the books on his desk into my back, jolting me forward. I felt a sharp pain shoot down my spine.

Mme. Larson switched to English. Very clearly she said, "In this class there are no excuses for getting out of doing your work."

The pain had gone away, but now I was fighting tears of frustration. My geometry teacher had been so sweet. "Take your time," she'd said, "I had a broken leg last summer. I know what you're going through. You can come in during my free period and I'll help you, or I can recommend a tutor." My biology teacher had welcomed me back, and the entire class had applauded my return.

"Mme. Larson." I managed to find my voice although it was very soft-spoken. "I've missed a lot of work—"

"I know," she interrupted. "You have a difficult three weeks in front of you as you prepare to take your

French final. I'll count your Jean Valjean presentation as one-half your grade to make it a bit more in your favor."

"But I thought I was exempt from the final!" I said. "I got an eighty-six on the midterm."

"But as you reminded me," she said, "you've missed so much work. How can I exempt you? I'd have no way of knowing if you caught up."

She didn't offer me extra help. She offered me extra work.

I never felt so tired or so angry in my life. But again, I held in my feelings. I couldn't lose it in school. If it weren't for the fact that my next class was English and Eric was in it, I'd have asked to be excused early.

After French class my friends gathered in the hall to complain sympathetically about Mme. Larson's unfairness.

The one good thing was that they didn't seem to notice my brace anymore. They weren't treating me like an outsider.

At first I didn't notice Eric standing there listening to all this. He took my books and led me through the crowded hall, guarding me from anyone charging recklessly down the corridor.

"I heard Larson is coming down pretty hard on you. You know, I'm in another of her classes. French is my best subject. Could I come over after school and help you catch up?"

"I didn't know you took French," I said, then added gratefully, "That would be very nice of you. I could really use the help." My mother was right, I thought. It could be okay to ask for help. It could be more than okay. It might even be romantic. "Thanks," I said.

"What are friends for?" Eric said, and he very gently put his hand on my shoulder, lump and all, and left it there.

Chapter Nine

It's Always Something

My mother picked up Michelle, Samantha, Andrea, and me at school. I could tell right away that something was wrong. She honked the horn at every moving object and muttered under her breath at several drivers. "I just got back from picking up your sister at Kennedy Airport. Flights are delayed and the traffic is a mess," she said. "I dropped her off at the house to unpack."

"How is she?" I asked.

"You'll see for yourself soon enough."

"I can't wait to see her," I said. Then I sighed. "I'm exhausted. My back is aching something fierce, and don't even ask about my French class."

"Oh, Carly. Was it a very tough day?" Mom's voice softened. "I can't believe I was so wound up about your sister that I didn't even ask how you were feeling."

"She did great," Michelle declared. "I carried her books for her."

"I'll carry your books anytime," Samantha offered. "I'd love to meet that jock who has an elevator pass. He had knee surgery or something. Talk about gorgeous! His name's Harris Walsh—isn't that a romantic name? I heard that he really is romantic, too, and brings his dates a single exotic flower—orchids usually. He works after school at the florist shop."

I saw Michelle take a deep breath and get starry-eyed. "Harris spoke to me today," she reported, and the others hung on her every word.

"What did he say?" Samantha asked.

"He said 'Excuse me' when he was getting off the elevator," Michelle said dreamily.

"'Excuse me' is not quite speaking to someone," Andrea said.

Michelle blushed.

"'Excuse me' definitely counts as speaking to someone. I was the witness. You had to be there," I said. "It was the *way* he said it."

"Well excuuuuuuuse me!" Andrea got huffy.

"So, what did you say back to him?" Samantha asked.

Michelle let out a giggle as she answered. "I didn't want to sound talkative or too interested. All I said was, 'Sure.'"

"'Sure' isn't even a sentence," Samantha said. "If I were there, I would have said, 'No room to move. Guess you'll just have to squeeze by.' And I would have looked straight into his eyes."

"No, you wouldn't," I defended Michelle. "You think you would have said that, but I know you. You would have thought that and said 'Sure' just like Michelle." I couldn't believe I was having this conversation. Just a few weeks ago I was worried about wiggling my toes and walking. Now I was arguing that "Excuse me" and "sure" was a real social exchange. It was kind of bizarre.

Mom dropped Samantha and Andrea off. I winced, turning too fast. I felt Michelle wince even more, as if she felt my pain, too. "I'm okay, Michelle," I said. "I just can't wait to get home and lie down."

"You should take a nap," Mom suggested.

"I don't need a nap. I'm not two years old. I just need to change my position, have some cookies and milk, and talk to my sister. I have so much to tell her." I didn't mean to snap at my mother. I guess the pain was getting to me, and the truth was a nap was a good idea, but I'd never let anyone know that. This was the real world, not the hospital. There was no time for naps.

"Your sister will have a lot to tell you," Mom warned. "Get the tissues ready."

"Just leave me alone with Pam for a while. She dried plenty of my tears when I was growing up. I owe her a few hundred tissues," I said.

I saw Michelle's quizzical look. "We'll talk and do homework later, okay?" I said.

"Sure." She helped me out of the car and carried my books inside. "Feel better."

"Don't worry, I will."

As I closed the door, I let out a holler. "PAM! Where are you?"

Pam came out of the living room. Her eyes were puffy and red. But she was still as beautiful as ever. She fell into my arms as if I were the strong one. I felt really good to be thought of that way. I patted her back and pushed the hair out of her eyes. "It's all right. Everything will be all right. You'll see." I repeated words she once used to comfort me when I lost the election for class president in grade school. I wanted to say something wise to her, but what kind of advice does a thirteen-year-old have to offer a twenty-four-year-old, almost divorced woman? I still wasn't used to her being married, and it was two years already. I certainly didn't feel old enough to have a sister getting ready for a divorce.

"Pam," I said, and hugged her some more. "I'm going to get right to the point like Tina, my roommate from the hospital, used to do. Are you getting a divorce, for sure? I've been so worried about you. Is there anything I can do?" I could see Pam's muscles relax as my own tensed. If I didn't sit down in the recliner chair soon, I thought I would break in half. I must have let out a grunt.

"Are you in pain?" Pam asked instead of answering my question.

"Just a bit, because I'm tired," I said, and took her hand to walk to the chair. "Come sit on the piano bench next to me." I sank into the chair and pushed the button that raised the footrest and lowered the back. "What a relief," I sighed.

Pam leaned over and stroked my forehead. "You poor baby. You must have been very frightened. I should have been at the hospital with you or at least sent flowers. I've been so self-absorbed. Not that I didn't worry about you. I did plenty of worrying, especially with Warren telling me he's known of cases like yours where the person never walked again. Real comforting, huh? Warren knows a medical horror story for almost every illness."

"You haven't answered my question," I interrupted. "Are you or aren't you getting a divorce?"

"Warren and I are growing apart. Yes, I think a divorce might be necessary." Pam sighed. "We're making each other miserable. We argue over everything."

"But can't you just talk things over? I can't believe this is happening," I said. "What happened to all the love and romance?"

"Of course we talk," Pam said. "I hate to disappoint you, sweetie, but communicating doesn't solve anything if nothing changes."

"But you two had to be pried apart before you were married. He took you to the nicest restaurants and shows. He bought you presents and sent you cards to tell you how much he loved you." Tears came to my eyes, and they weren't from back pain. "My sister, divorced? I can't believe it."

"Now, Warren thinks the best restaurant is our kitchen with me doing the cooking. The only note he leaves these days says, 'Don't forget to pick up my shirts.' "

"But you were so in love with him. Did you fall out of love? Is love just a big joke?"

"I don't think we were ever in love," Pam admitted. "I think we were infatuated with each other and Warren had a way with words. My heart would pound at the sight of him. We were in love with love and not each other."

"Then why did you get married? Marriage is supposed to be forever."

"We wanted the glamour and romance of a beautiful wedding and honeymoon. Then one day we woke up and the sink was filled with dishes, the apartment needed to be vacuumed, and we both had to go to work. Don't ever marry anyone you've known for only six months."

"Don't worry," I said, "I'm not in love. But I think I'm infatuated. There was this eighteen-year-old guy, Jess, in the hospital. The sight of him made my heart pound, too."

"But do you know anything about him?" Pam asked.

"Well..." I thought for a moment and then answered, "He made me laugh and forget my pain. And he didn't let little things bother him." I left out the part about all the girls visiting him. "I gave him my address but I don't think he'll write. He didn't give me his."

"It's just as well," Pam said. "He sounds nice, but maybe he's too old for you. Don't you like anyone your own age?"

"There's this guy, Eric, who I always smiled at in school." I paused. "I guess he must have noticed because he surprised me and visited me in the hospital. We'd never even gone on a date."

"You do have a really great smile," Pam said. "You always did, even as a baby. It's so good to talk things over with you. I'm glad I came home."

I reached for her hand. "I'm glad you're home, too."

Pam's eyes filled with tears. "You know," she said,

"part of my problem with Warren has to do with babies."

"You mean you're pregnant? I'm going to be an aunt? That's great! I love babies." In my excitement I squeezed Pam's hand.

"Calm down, Carly." Pam moved her hand away from mine and rubbed where her engagement ring had dug in. "No, I'm not pregnant. Just the opposite. I wasn't going to tell you all this. I know Mom and Dad want to be grandparents, but I really don't want to have a baby right now."

"And Warren does?"

"He's really pressuring me. If I hear him say, 'It's time to have a baby' once more, I'll scream."

I couldn't believe that my sister, who had played with dolls till she got a bra, didn't want a baby. I felt a little disappointed that I wasn't going to be an aunt after all, but I was glad she'd confided in me. "What do you tell Warren?"

"I told him, 'Wait a minute. I don't even know if our marriage is working. Becoming a parent is a very serious decision. We both have to be ready.' I want a baby very much—someday, but not now. My advertising career is moving along and Warren's busy building his practice. He's hardly home. You don't save a marriage by having a baby—it's not that simple."

"Is romance and advertising more important?"

"What are you, a psychiatrist?" she asked me.

"At least you can do something, get professional help maybe, and save your marriage, right?"

"You can always do something to help any problem."

"Not always," I said. "Sometimes you can't even help yourself wiggle your toes even if it's for the most important reason of all . . . to walk." As I said that, half out loud and half to myself, something clicked inside my mind. I started to see the problems around me in order. Pam's problem was in the middle. Not as important as worrying about surgery and walking, but definitely more important than my problem about losing touch with Jess and Tina. And maybe a speck more important than Dad's business problems. But not as important as my disappointment in him. Where did my speech in French fit in? I'd have to think about that some more.

Pam went on, too worried about her own problems, I guess, to hear about mine. "Sometimes I really need my family," she said. "Maybe I should just move back home."

"You might want to think twice about that. Things aren't terrific here, either. Personally, I'd love to have you back. Mom and Dad are absolutely hyper from your problems and my problems and their own business problems. I don't know what to do anymore, except leave notes that say "Dear Mom and Dad, don't worry." I don't understand it. Parents are supposed to be able to handle everybody's problems. They're not supposed to fall apart. You know Daddy never came into the hospital room to stay with me for longer than two minutes? He couldn't even stay long enough to give me a hug."

"I didn't know that," she said. "I didn't even know they were having business problems. I guess it's easier for them to spare me when all our conversations are long distance."

"Sometimes I think maybe Mom and Dad need to be babied a bit, like they used to do for us when we were upset. Remember?"

"I remember. Extra hugs and kisses, treats under our pillows, or a nice note in our lunch boxes. You may be right. Let's think about what we should do." She reached over to rumple up my hair. "So how's school going?"

"I have to translate and read this simplified excerpt from a French novel, *Les Misérables*, and then I actually have to make a speech in French, in front of the class. I think I'll die."

"I'm not too up on my French, but I could try to help."

"Well, actually, I have to admit I got a better offer— from Eric. I think he likes me. The day he traveled all the way to the country to visit me at the hospital, he even brought me some flowers."

"He sounds very thoughtful," Pam said. "I can't believe my baby sister is talking about boys and love and romance. When I left home, boys weren't on your mind half as much as collecting stickers or charms with Michelle."

"Yeah, well, I've grown up even faster since I was in the hospital. Now I think about more than just love and romance. It's as if I'm seeing the world for the first time. Flowers are more beautiful and people look so graceful when they walk fast or jump over a puddle. And things I would have gotten crazy about before, like a stain on a blouse I wanted to wear, seem so silly now. So many things are just not important compared to being able to walk. And friends and family are more important than ever before. I took so much for granted without realizing it."

This time Pam listened and didn't interrupt my long thought. Then she said, "You sound so serious. That's okay, but don't forget to laugh at things, too."

We both faked a laugh. "Let's bake chocolate chip cookies while you're here, the way we used to. Okay?" I asked.

"Okay."

I noticed that Pam only used up three tissues during this talk, so I figured maybe I helped her a bit. She wasn't cheerful, but at least she wasn't crying.

The telephone rang and she went to answer it. I wondered if she was hoping it was Warren. "It's for you, Carly," she called from the next room.

I automatically answered, "Tell Michelle to come over in an hour and we'll get to work studying. I just need to rest a bit first. I don't feel like getting up to talk."

"What did you say?" Pam called. "I didn't catch all of it. 'Come over in an hour'—was that it?"

"Yes," I called back.

Pam came back in the room. "He sounds nice," she said.

"Who sounds nice?"

"The boy who's coming over in an hour to help you with your French homework. Eric."

"That was Eric on the phone? Not Michelle?"

"Yes."

"He's coming over in an hour?"

"I told him just what you told me to say. Yes, he'll be over in an hour."

I pushed the button on the recliner chair and practically ejected myself out of it. "What am I going to do with my hair! It looks absolutely atrocious!"

Pam laughed for the first time.

"Hair I still worry about," I said. "I guess I'm not all grown-up."

"Hair, I'm still good at."

"You have to help get me ready," I pleaded.

"Sure. What else are big sisters for?"

"I love you," I said, and she reached for another tissue. "Did you ever think you'd hear me say that when I was spying on you or screaming at you when we were younger and you touched one of my things?"

"Never," she said, "although I always knew deep down that I loved you—even though you were a huge pain."

We walked toward my room. Pam's arm rested around my shoulder. As we passed Mom, I saw her smile for the first time in a long time.

I called out to her, "Emergency hair repairs. It's always something. Eric's coming over."

Chapter Ten

There's Romance
and There's Romance

Exactly one hour later the doorbell rang. I wondered if Eric had actually arrived early and waited outside until it was exactly an hour. He's so perfect. His blond hair looked combed and his clothes looked freshly ironed even after he'd worn them all day at school. My heart wasn't pounding, but I was glad to see him.

"I brought the tape from the musical production of *Les Misérables* to put us in the mood," he said.

"Sounds good to me."

My first problem, I thought, was where should we work. If it were Michelle, we would have gone straight to my room, kicked my pajamas and other assorted laundry aside, and spread our books and papers on the floor or the bed. I'd never studied with a boy before. Pam was staying in the den, which had former-ly been her room. Mom was in the kitchen. That left the dining room or living room. "Come on into the living room," I said, since we were practically in it anyway.

My second problem was not wanting to look dumb, yet being so behind in French that he'd have to keep coming to tutor me.

My third problem was my mother and sister. They winked and snickered at each other as they came in to bring us pretzels, popcorn, and soda. They had that "Isn't he cute, aren't they adorable" look on their faces. And there was nothing I could do about it. If I said anything to them, it would just make their behavior more obvious to Eric.

"I don't know where to begin on this speech," I said after Pam and Mom left the room.

"At the beginning," Eric said, very much in control. "There are fifteen pages in this excerpt of *Les Misérables*. If we take turns reading, translating, and talking about the story, you'll get an idea for your speech. You'll see."

My fourth problem, I found, was concentrating on French when I was sitting so close to Eric to share the book. If we turned to look at each other, we'd practically be kissing.

As Eric read the French, I translated the words into English, stopping now and then to look up the meaning of a word in my French dictionary. I liked listening to Eric pronouncing French words. I'd never enjoyed studying so much before. After five pages, we stopped to review the material we'd covered.

"So far Jean Valjean has stolen some bread to feed his sister's starving family," Eric began.

I continued, "After nineteen years in prison, he's out. But people are still rotten to him except for a bishop who helps him. Valjean changes his name and becomes successful because he invents something.

"He becomes an entrepreneur," I added, "starting his own business."

"He even goes on to become mayor of his town in France," Eric picked up when I left off, moving even closer to me, if that was possible. "He helps a lot of people and is very respected. Then this detective Javert figures out that this Mayor Madeleine is really Jean Valjean, the convict."

Eric reached over me to get a handful of popcorn. If anyone walked in, they would definitely think we were sitting on the couch making out. I wished for a moment that Jean Valjean would take a flying leap and leave Eric and me free for flirting and romance. Then as I felt his hand gently move on my shoulder past the lump of the brace to where I could feel his touch, I realized that the way he was taking time to help me, really help me, not just showing off how much he knew, was really pretty romantic in its way.

"What do we know about Jean Valjean so far that would be good in a speech?" Eric asked, and waited patiently for my answer.

I looked into his eyes. They looked hopeful and encouraging. I think he was looking at me lovingly. Was that possible? His eyes sort of glistened and sparkled as he gazed at me, and I wondered if my eyes were doing the same thing.

I forced my mind back onto Jean Valjean and said, "Well, we know he feels bad about people suffering, and he believes in fairness. And the story shows that when you're very poor, even good people may do something illegal to save their families. But they can become honest again, take their punishment, and help others."

"You could write a terrific speech on any of those ideas," Eric said.

I was beginning to believe him. More important, his encouragement was making me believe more in myself. We discussed the next five pages, ending at the place where Mayor Madeleine hears of how a homeless person has been charged not only with stealing some fruit, but also of being Jean Valjean, a convict. The man is on trial. Only the mayor knows the man is innocent, because he himself is really Valjean. Would he give away his true identity and lose his good reputation?

I was really getting interested in this story. It took my mind off my back pain, self-consciousness about the brace, my family's problems—everything.

As I relaxed, Eric and I turned toward each other at the same moment—and just as I had thought, our lips were touching. Just then the doorbell rang. Why did we have to be interrupted at probably the most romantic moment of my life? I leaped up at the sound and we smashed noses—not exactly romantic! I don't think that would have happened to Judy and Dr. Ginario. For all I know, I thought, I could have broken Eric's nose, the way he was clutching it. Pam opened the door.

"Pam, hi!" I heard Michelle's greeting.

"Michelle, you're so grown-up," Pam answered.

Michelle walked into the room, took in the scene, and said, "I'm sorry. I didn't know you had company. Want me to come back later?"

"No, stay," I said. "Eric's been helping me decipher *Les Misérables*. We got a lot done already."

"Well, I better be on my way." Eric got up and walked to the door. "See you in school tomorrow." Then he whispered, "Studying with you was fun."

"Thanks," I said.

I closed the door. "I can't believe I didn't tell him I had a good time, too."

"Well, what did you say?" Michelle asked.

"I didn't say anything."

"Maybe when you're scared, you can't say what you want to say," Michelle said.

"Maybe. Anyway, I think Eric and I just had a romantic moment."

"You did?"

We curled up on the couch, ate popcorn, and talked. "Maybe romance is not all about thumping hearts and gifts of single long-stemmed roses," I said to her.

"My heart would definitely thump if Harris Walsh turned to me in the elevator and gave me a single long-stemmed rose. That would definitely be the most romantic moment of my life—just like in books and movies and TV. Romance is romance," Michelle said.

"I don't think so. I used to think that, but now I think there's romance and there's romance. There are lots of little things that are much more romantic and that you don't see in movies and on TV."

"Like what?" Michelle asked.

"Like Eric's offering to help me with French without my even asking him. Like practically kissing accidentally because we were sitting so close together and turning suddenly and crashing noses." I laughed at the memory.

"That's not romance," Michelle argued. "Romance is things like gifts of candy or flowers and sparks flying when fingers touch and stuff like that."

"But Eric made my heart pound a little bit, by helping me."

"Pounding a little bit doesn't count. You were probably just nervous about the speech."

"I disagree. If a person's heart pounds a little bit and wants to pound more about a certain person, then something romantic must have happened."

"Did Eric kiss you? Is that what I interrupted?" Michelle asked.

"Yeah, sort of," I started, then emphatically said, "Yes."

"Was it a great kiss?"

"I guess. I think there are different kinds of romance like there are different kinds of people. Like Jess in the hospital. He was a flirty kind of romance that was just part of him as much as the way he dressed or breathed. He could make people laugh and feel good and that was romantic."

"I didn't meet Jess, so I can't agree or disagree," Michelle said. "Let's take a known case. Warren used to call Pam a lot and bring her flowers and presents and make candlelight dinners for her. He was so perfect."

"Guess again," I said. "Mr. Perfect is a fink. Pam is home because she's thinking of divorcing him."

"Why? He's got everything. Good looks, a good job. They always had so much fun together." Michelle looked shocked.

"I guess people change, or maybe they sometimes pretend to be someone they're not by using romance like a mask to get what they want."

"I can't believe your sister is getting a divorce," Michelle interrupted.

"*May* be getting a divorce. It's not definite yet," I corrected her.

"I thought Pam and Warren would be married forever and have candlelight dinners when they were eighty years old."

"Maybe we read too many fairy tales when we were kids," I said. "Before my accident I probably would have agreed with you. Have I changed?"

Michelle looked me over. "You look exactly the same."

"You can't see inside me, though," I whispered.

"Well, you do have a lot more opinions." Michelle didn't sound too happy about that.

We both got up. I took the empty popcorn bowl and put it in the dishwasher. Mom and Pam were sitting at the kitchen table sipping coffee. There was a box of tissues set up between them, and they each had a wad in their hands. They greeted us and stopped talking while we were in the room.

93

"Everything is so serious," I said. "Let's lighten things up around this house."

Pam reached over and flicked on the light. "That's the best I can do right now," she said. "I just got off the phone with Romeo. The problem is, he'll be Warren by the time I get home."

"Are you going back to Chicago?" I asked. "You just got here."

"I have to go back to see if we can work things out. We're going to see a marriage counselor, so at least we'll know we tried. I don't want to feel guilty over not having tried hard enough. Especially when it's something as important as this." At the mention of the word "guilty," I noticed Michelle got jittery. "Anyway, I can only take off a couple of days before the ad agency falls apart without me."

"Carly, don't you think you should rest up and take a nap now?" Mom said. "You look exhausted. Pam, you should lie down, too. You'll need your strength."

"You look tired yourself, Ma," I said softly. "Don't wear yourself out."

"I was up most of the night. Your father was worried about me and I was worried about him. We spent the night cheering each other up. Now I'd like to get down to the store so he can get out and look for a new place for the business. By the way, Pam and I think your Eric is real cute."

"I gathered that," I said. "But he's not *my* Eric."

Michelle and I went to my room to continue our discussion. "I've got another couple to add to our romantic-couples list," Michelle said.

94

"Who?"

"Your parents."

"My parents?"

"Yeah," she said. "I think the way they help each other out during tough times and work together in the store is very romantic."

"I never thought about it before," I said. "But I think you might be right." Just realizing that my parents still had romance in their marriage made me feel better.

Chapter Eleven

Follow the Advice
of Your Heart

In school the next week Michelle started passing me notes with symbols instead of boys' names in case they got into the wrong hands.

C—

In geometry today (?) was funny. We had a sub so we didn't do much. I was telling Andrea that you were going to get your hair cut, and (?) told me that he hadn't gotten his hair cut for six months. Now he really talked to me, much more than "excuse me." I'm going to do it. In the elevator tomorrow I'm going to give him a single long-stemmed rose and see what happens. What have I got to lose? My life, that's what. I'll die of embarrassment if he doesn't take it.

M.

I wrote notes back to her. We slipped them to each

97

other in the hall or in the few classes we were in together. I wrote:

M—

It sounds to me like (?) may be starting to think of you in a new way. (!) waits for me after each class. Today he held my hand as we walked through the hall. (!) is coming over again tomorrow afternoon to help me with my Jean Valjean speech. Yesterday we finished reading and translating. The French excerpt from *Les Misérables* turns out to be the best love story. (!) read Marius's lines and I read Cosette's. It definitely was very romantic without flowers or candy. I rest my case. But good luck with (?) and the rose. Only he might be embarrassed to take the rose in the elevator, with people watching.

C.

In French, after class, Mme. Larson asked me if I was ready to give my speech on Monday. My heart started to pound at the thought. There's definitely a difference between a person's heart pounding with nervousness and pounding with romance, I thought.

"I might need an extra day or two." I managed to get the words out, although I felt as if they were stuck in my throat.

"You'll have an extra day or two to prepare," she said.

I looked up, surprised at her kindness.

Then she added, "Saturday and Sunday."

One of Mom's expressions popped into my mind: "She gives you ice in winter."

At home Pam and I sat at the kitchen table and planned a special dinner for Mom and Dad. "I'm nervous about leaving in the morning," Pam said.

"I'll miss you," I answered.

We walked to the avenue together and picked up Chinese food and a chocolate cake from the bakery. I don't know which smelled better. It felt good to be encouraged to walk and even asked to carry a package.

"I'm glad you don't baby me like Mom and Dad do." I could feel the warmth of the Chinese food against me as I spoke.

"Speaking of Dad," Pam said, "he called before. He sounded excited about something. He didn't ask if you got off to school all right or if Warren had called me today. He just said he and Mom would be home as early as possible. I told him we planned dinner. You would have thought I'd given him a million dollars."

"It must have been nice to hear Daddy sound happy. It's been a while," I said.

I guess Pam is so busy with her own crisis, she can't deal with anyone else's, I thought. She didn't ask me more about Dad.

"Oh, let's stop off at the drugstore. I want to get some perfume," Pam said.

"Are you preparing to package yourself for Romeo?"

"Well, there is this perfume I used to wear that he always loved. He probably won't even notice it or else it will make him sneeze. But I'm going to give this marriage one last shot."

"Do you want it to work out? Do you still love him?"

"I'm very mixed up," she said. "Since I've been here, he's called and sent me a little stuffed bear that says 'I Miss You.' And he didn't add anything about having a baby. On the phone he tells me how he misses my soft skin. He hasn't talked to me like that in a long time."

"As long as he doesn't tell you, 'Your teeth are like stars—they come out at night,'" I joked.

Pam laughed. "That's one of Daddy's old fifties jokes," she said. "Remember the days when he used to joke about just about anything?"

"Yeah," I said, and wished that could happen again.

Pam paid the salesclerk, who made a point of rating the perfume as one of her own favorites and I guess therefore an excellent choice. We stopped at the corner candy store to buy a newspaper for Dad.

"Look at those pink rubber balls," I said, pointing to a box in the window.

"I haven't bounced a ball in ages," Pam said. "I'm buying one for us."

"Great idea."

We walked the rest of the way, put the food in the refrigerator, and then bounced the ball off the porch stoop, catching it on a fly to get points.

"I'm not doing very well, but that's because I'm holding myself back," I joked. "Seriously, I'm trying to play stoop ball in moderation, like Dr. Ginario advised."

"You should take it easy," Pam said. "I forgot you probably shouldn't be chasing after balls."

"I know. It was great that you forgot. It was good to feel normal again, even for just a couple of minutes."

We went into the house very sweaty and very happy.

I picked up the mail from the floor under the mail slot. I forgot how tough it was to straighten up again. At least it was worth the effort. One of the envelopes was addressed to me. I put the newspaper down on the piano bench next to the reclining chair. This evening I'd let Dad sit in his own chair instead of collapsing in it myself. I decided to rest in it for just a few minutes and open my mail. Maybe it was a letter from Jess. There was no return address. I read the words on the front of the card:

Hope it brightens up your day
   just receiving this card from me.

Then inside it said:

I know it brightens up mine
   sending it to you.

                                                    Eric

I was surprised to see Eric's name, not Jess's. I closed my eyes to think more deeply. Eric sent a card especially for me. It was better than if he'd clipped a rose from a bush.

The next thing I knew Mom and Dad were home. I

was waking up slowly, not moving a muscle, when I heard Dad practically whisper to my mom, "She looks so helpless. It breaks my heart. I can't deal with it."

"Just don't break her heart in the process," Mom said to him. "She needs you now. Don't forget that."

"I know. That's why I'm going to call that center that Dr. Ginario recommended to help me deal with this anxiety."

I pretended to sleep so they wouldn't know I heard them. My father was going to see someone especially to help him cope with me? I wasn't sure how I felt. Angry to be thought of as a crisis to be coped with. Sad for breaking his heart. Annoyed that he couldn't stop thinking about himself and the way everything made him feel. If he would just take a minute to reach out and touch my hand or kiss my forehead like he used to . . . But I was happy that he was trying as best he could to do something about it. I felt proud of Mom for reminding him of my feelings and needs in all this. Mothers are funny, I thought. They understand a lot more than you think, only they keep it a secret.

After a couple of minutes I got up and wandered, yawning and stretching, into the kitchen. The table was set and Pam put the Chinese food in the microwave.

"What a nice treat," Dad said, peeking into the glass oven door. "You ordered my favorites, even though no one else likes moo shu and chicken and peanuts in hot sauce."

"We got wonton soup, chow mein, and egg rolls for us regulars," I said. "Don't worry, we won't starve."

Dad reached out for my hand and held it. I almost

cried at his touch. Okay, so it was over chicken and peanuts in hot sauce, but I counted it as a meaningful moment anyway. I reached back to hug him, but he was already seating himself and watching Pam place the moo shu in front of him. I got the chicken and brought it to him instead.

"What wonderful girls we have," he said to Mom as if we were little again.

"The best," Mom agreed, and Pam and I exchanged glances, pleased with ourselves for planning this special dinner.

"I actually have some good news to tell you," Dad said. "And this is such a good moment to tell you. It's not often we're here like this, just the four of us. It makes it extraspecially nice for me."

"Great," I said. "What's the news?"

"I've found a new location for the store. It's even got two windows and a big storeroom for merchandise. There's enough room to buy in quantity and get better prices so we'll be able to manage the higher rent. And if business goes well and if I can get the bank to back me, I might be able to buy the building one of these days."

"Dad, that's terrific," Pam said.

"You can do anything you set your mind to," Mom encouraged him.

"That's super. I'm glad you found a new place so fast," I said.

"You should only know," Mom said.

"What do you mean?" I asked. "It's only been a few weeks of serious looking, right?"

"More like three months," Dad said, "with one deal falling through because I couldn't get back to the realtor in time. Things came up."

"You never told me you were having such problems," I said. "Was it my accident, the thing that came up?"

"It doesn't matter," Mom said. "You had enough trouble of your own."

"You were in no condition to be burdened with our problems," Dad said.

"Hey, guys, it's all solved now anyway," Pam interrupted.

"But if I knew, I would have understood things better," I said. "It's hard enough to figure out what's the more important crisis to get through when you know the whole story. I'm a teenager now. You have to let me help you, too." Then I dropped the subject, not wanting to spoil the evening.

Dad was thinking of the future, I thought happily, and dreaming of success instead of doom and gloom— at least about business. Before my accident I probably wouldn't have noticed. Now I even hear the words people are trying not to say. Maybe I learned that from listening to Dr. Ginario not say the word "surgery."

The best part of dinner was the fortune cookies. We all made a big deal about who got which one and who read theirs first. It felt so good to be laughing and joking together as a family, all four of us.

Mom read her fortune first: " 'Share your happiness with others today.' . . . Very nice. I am very happy and I share it with all of you."

"Thanks for my share of your happiness." I gave her a hug.

Dad went next. " 'Enjoy what you have. Hope for what you lack.' . . . Sounds so simple. Why is it so hard to do that?" he asked, not really expecting an answer.

I answered anyway, "Maybe sometimes we get too worried to enjoy anything." I didn't look at him. I looked down at my own fortune cookie.

Pam's fortune cracked us all up. " 'Listen not to vain words of empty tongue.' . . . What on earth does that mean?" she said, laughing.

"If it had said 'empty head,' I would have thought it meant the way Warren's been treating you," I said.

"That's not a very nice thing to say." Suddenly she was defending Warren.

"Sorry," I said, surprised. "I thought you would laugh."

"I guess I'm oversensitive. I'm hoping, now that I'm going back, that his words and gifts haven't been fooling me."

"Going to a marriage counselor can't hurt," Mom said.

"I think you're doing the right thing," Dad agreed.

"You can always come home again if it doesn't work out," I added. Mom wasn't too thrilled at my remark.

I read my fortune cookie last. I like the suspense. My fortune cookie said, "Follow the advice of your heart." I thought of Jess and I thought of Eric. My heart pounded at both thoughts. Just what I needed. A confused heart to listen to.

The phone rang and I automatically got up to answer it. Things felt so normal tonight. No one insisted I sit still and rest.

It was Eric. He asked me if I got the card. I thanked him. I should have said more, but I couldn't find the words.

"That was Eric. He asked me out on a date to the movies on Friday night," I announced to my family, returning to the kitchen.

"That'll be nice," Mom said, and the others agreed.

Now there was something to look forward to, a real date. What movie would we see? What would I wear? Would he put his arm around me? Thinking about Eric helped me not think scary thoughts about giving my speech in French. And as my back ached, one buried question kept creeping into my mind. Would my X rays show that I needed surgery?

Chapter Twelve

All You Can Do Is
the Best You Can Do

I'm not the nail-biting type. But now, suddenly,
every time I sat down to work on my Jean Valjean
speech, my fingernails popped right into my mouth. I
knew I was supernervous.

"Just begin. Write one paragraph today," Eric encouraged me as we said good-bye after classes. "I have
to talk myself into starting projects," he admitted.
"Then once I get going, I'm okay." I could hardly hear
him over the noise of kids shouting to each other and
hustling out of the building.

"One paragraph doesn't sound as bad as a whole
speech." I practically had to shout to be heard.

"I'll call you tonight and you can read it to me," Eric
said. "It may be late. I'll be working at my dad's
pharmacy."

Michelle decided to see if Harris would ask about
her if she wasn't with me on the elevator. Samantha
eagerly carried my books instead. When Mom picked
us up today, I knew immediately what Michelle meant
when she said, "So?"

"He didn't say a word to me about you. Aren't you

glad that you took my advice and didn't give him the rose?"

"He didn't even ask where I was?" Michelle was not letting my words compute.

"He's in his own world, Michelle," I said. "He's used to being looked at, not looking."

"When did you get so smart?" Mom asked. I didn't think she was listening. Usually her mind is on a million things, and even when I'm talking directly to her, she'll ask a question I just answered.

"April twenty-fifth. That's when I got so smart," I joked back. "Eight thirty-five to be exact."

"I can see you're feeling better these days," she said. "I'm glad to hear your smart answers again."

"Let's get together and we'll plan my next move," Michelle said.

"Maybe later," I said. "I absolutely have to finish my Jean Valjean speech today. But I'll assign a part of my brain to think about you and Harris. Okay?"

"Okay."

Mom dropped us off and drove on to the store to help pack up for the big move. This morning I'd offered to help, but they wouldn't hear of it. I could still hear Dad's words in my mind: "Thanks, honey, but not with your back. We don't want to look for trouble now, do we? All you need to do is lift something the wrong way. Who knows what might happen? I'd never forgive myself."

I think about things so much more these days. Why can't people forgive themselves? I thought now, and that gave me an idea for my speech. Jean Valjean wasn't able to forgive himself either. I thought of Eric's advice to just start and write a paragraph. I didn't even stop for cookies and milk. I grabbed a pencil and paper and took them to the reclining chair. Scribbling away as fast as I could, I wrote in English because I'd never be able to think that fast in French. It would be added work to translate everything, and I tried to keep my sentences simple, but my thoughts started to lead the way and I just followed with my pencil. The important thing at this late date was to have something to say. Anything. "All you can do is the best you can do." Another Mom saying came to mind. I wrote:

> If Jean Valjean were here today, he'd be the first one to tell you he's a thief. He wouldn't ask to get away with it. He stole a loaf of bread to feed his sister's seven starving children. He served many years in prison for it but still lived the rest of his life feeling like a criminal. He wasn't able to forgive himself. Why is that so hard to do? It's terrible to see hungry children. I can understand how such a terrible sight might have made him do something he'd rather not have done. Sometimes you don't know what you'll do when you see something terrible.

The paragraph was finished, but I wasn't. Thoughts from deep inside me were coming up to the surface, like when you jump in the lake and let yourself rise to the top. I continued to write. How much of it I'd use in my speech would depend on how much I could translate. I read:

> In the story *Les Misérables*, Jean Valjean takes an orphaned child, Cosette, and raises her. He makes a good life for both of them even though he's hunted down by a detective, Javert, who thinks justice is served only when Jean Valjean is imprisoned. But people can change and learn and help others even if they had a bad start. People should be able to forgive themselves and others and grow.

Eric called around eleven P.M. Funny, I didn't feel at all embarrassed to read him what I'd written. I trusted him. I guess that means I like him a lot.

"That's really good, Carly." Eric didn't laugh at me or make me feel dumb. I wondered if I could have read my speech to Jess. "I hope between the two of us we know enough French to make it make sense," he added.

"I know what you mean." I fidgeted to find a comfortable position for sitting up in my bed. "I once wrote this paragraph in French and read it out loud. Every time I thought I was saying 'hair,' I was saying 'horses' because *cheveux* and *chevaux* are almost the same. So I described washing and combing my horse, getting it cut short, and putting the pieces in an envelope to save for my scrap book. It really sounded gross. Mme. Larson did a number on me. She had the whole class laughing. I left the room as fast as I could so I wouldn't cry in class." Why was I telling Eric all this? He didn't have to know I'd been embarrassed like that. I never talked this way to a boy before.

"That must have been awful for you," he said with such understanding in his voice that I felt my heart melting. I suddenly realized that this talking honestly was very romantic.

"You think that's embarrassing," Eric continued, "I once had to give a report in social studies and my voice was changing. Every other sentence sounded like someone else with a high-pitched voice was speaking." He demonstrated and laughed.

"I bet you felt like you wanted the earth to swallow you up. But just think how now, a year or so later, you're probably the only one who remembers it happened."

"Yeah," he said, "but at least I had a good teacher. He wouldn't allow the class to laugh at me. He even said how that had happened to him and would probably happen to a lot of the boys in the class sooner or later."

"Carly, are you still on the phone?" Dad called in to me.

"It's important. It's homework," I announced. "Does that line work in your house, too?" I asked Eric.

"Every time," he answered, and we laughed. "At least homework comes in handy for something. Oh, before I forget, is there any special movie you wanted to see Friday night?"

"Anything, as long as it doesn't scare me to death and give me nightmares," I said. "I hate those pictures that bleed all over the screen."

"Good, because I'd be the first to have the nightmare myself. Hang on a minute, my mother's calling me."

As I waited, I thought to myself that I liked the way Eric could be honest about himself and not put on a big brave act. I wondered if Jess could do that. Then I wondered why I keep wondering about Jess. I never heard a word from him. Neither did Tina. I'd sent her a note and she'd sent me a card back. One of these days I'll write her again.

"So I'll pick out the movie and hope you haven't seen it. We can always switch plans later," Eric said when he returned to the phone.

But I knew I would rather see a movie twice than tell. I wanted Eric to feel good about planning the date.

"I'm glad I'll be with you this weekend. I'm going to be a nervous wreck about giving this speech on Monday," I said.

"It's great. You'll do fine. I know you will."

After we said good-bye and hung up, I felt this warm, wonderful feeling deep inside. Like knowing someone was believing in me. His thinking of me and planning a date for me was so special.

I called Michelle to tell her about this romantic moment and help her plan her next move with Harris. We came up with five words for her to say to him: "Did you miss me yesterday?"

The problem is, what if he says no?

Chapter Thirteen

That Should Be
Your Worst Problem

I phoned Michelle four times in one hour deciding
and redeciding what I should wear on my date with
Eric. Six blouses, two pairs of jeans, and a skirt were
piled on top of my bed, which looked like the bargain
table in a department store. Finally, Michelle just came
over and stood in front of my closet with me.

"Why is going out on a date with Eric making me so
nervous?" I asked.

"You're excited, that's all," Michelle answered. "You
want everything to be perfect. Relax and be yourself."

"Everything I try on today seems to make my brace
look even lumpier than usual."

"You notice the lumps because you're looking for
them," Michelle said.

"My first date with Eric and I probably won't even
feel it if he puts his arm around me at the movies. Why
did this have to happen to me?" Michelle looked awful
when I said that, but I couldn't help how I felt. I didn't
blame her for what happened, but I had to get my
feelings out in the open, too. "I can't find anything to

wear!" I threw the semi-sheer blouse I had in my hands into the air.

"Carly, that should be your worst problem," my mother called from the kitchen.

"Please stop saying that to me!" I shouted back. "It *is* my worst problem right now. I know, I'm lucky I can walk. You don't have to say it. But I haven't completely grown up overnight!"

"Wear this," Michelle interrupted, and handed me a turquoise cotton jumpsuit with shoulder pads that I'd forgotten about. I tried it on. It really did the trick.

"You saved me, Michelle." I threw my arms around her.

I got dressed and carefully put on my makeup. "Wear blue eye shadow," Michelle said.

"Okay. I'll put on a little extra so it will make my eyes sparkle in the dark movie theater."

"Good idea," Michelle agreed.

She gave me a good-luck hug before she left. "You look beautiful," she said. "Eric will be here any minute, so I'll get lost. Call me later."

"I will. Thanks for your help."

I was in a good mood until I walked into the kitchen. "You look beautiful," Mom said, "except...how can you keep your eyes open with the weight of all that eye shadow on your lids?"

"I want it to show up in the dark," I explained.

"Take some of it off," Mom said firmly.

"Why?" I argued.

"Because I said so...and I'm the mother."

"My favorite answer." I groaned and went back to

my room and took off some eye shadow, but not too much.

"Now you look terrific!" Mom said, peeking into my room.

I noticed one thing that felt great. Mom had yelled at me as just Carly, not Carly with the broken back. Only Michelle still treated me differently. I wished I could do something about that. But what?

The doorbell rang, interrupting my thoughts. I tried to beat Dad to the door, but he was too quick for me. He surprised me by letting out a wolf whistle. "You look lovely, Carly!" he said. After my blush faded, I felt really happy that he'd noticed and said something.

Eric came in and greeted everyone. "Dad, this is Eric." I introduced them. "Eric, this is my dad," I said, as if he'd never have figured it out.

Mom came into the living room. I noticed she'd put lipstick on and combed her hair. A couple of minutes ago she'd looked like she'd walked through a windstorm.

"Eric. How nice to see you again," she said, beaming her pleasure. Eric would probably think I never had a date before. Well, I haven't had many, I thought, but there were school dances and stuff, and each time my father did this interviewing as if I were going to marry the guy. I knew that when I got home he'd explain, as usual, how important it was to know whom your child is going off with. Someone should teach parents how to act relaxed and casual when a date comes to pick up their daughter.

When my father got to "What do you plan to study in college?" I knew it was time to be going.

"Electronics engineering," Eric answered in a flash. That was news to me. He seemed so sure of himself.

"Good field," Mom said. I wondered how or if she knew that for a fact. I also realized we'd miss the beginning of the movie if we didn't get out of here soon, and I hate that.

"Time to go," I announced, getting up.

Eric walked fast, maybe because he's tall and I'm short. I practically had to take three steps to his every one.

We walked to the avenue and took a bus to the movie theater on Kings Highway where the latest James Bond movie was playing.

I hadn't been to a movie theater since my accident. I never realized the seats were so narrow. I squeezed into my seat. My brace took up more room than I thought. I could also tell by the ache in my back that it would probably be raining, maybe even thundering and lightning when we got out. These days, I thought, I could predict weather better than a TV weatherperson.

Was my back getting worse? I should call Dr. Ginario and ask if I should still feel this pain. But what if it means I need surgery? No, I told myself. I'm on a date. I'm going to have fun tonight and not sit and worry!

The movie was exciting. Eric was enjoying it as much for the inventions and contraptions as for the beautiful women. I was watching him enjoy it. I especially liked when he found a spot on my neck to tickle with his finger. Then he put his arm all the way around my shoulders and ran his fingers up and down my arm. He made me forget I even wore a brace. We shared popcorn, and when he kissed me, he tasted buttery and salty.

One problem—what to do with two unpopped kernels I tossed into my mouth with a handful of popped ones. I figured it was not too cool to spit on a date or dig in my mouth with a finger when they got caught in my retainer. I tried to free them with my tongue, feeling glad the theater was dark. I must have looked like I was trying out for a funny-face contest, not like someone on an important date. Finally, the kernels were freed, and I crunched them. It sounded to me that everyone could hear me as the crunching noise echoed in my head.

Eric turned to me and said, "You like the unpopped corn, too? We have something in common." He popped a few into his mouth and crunched away. He made me feel so relaxed.

I was right. It was pouring when we got outside. All the careful attention to my makeup and hair would be washed away before we walked a block.

"We're going to get wet anyway, so we might as well enjoy ourselves," Eric said, taking my hand. "I loved to splash through puddles as a kid. Still do." He put his foot down hard in the puddle in front of us.

"I was a splasher, too," I said. "I guess we have a couple of things in common."

We splashed and dripped and laughed our way home. "I had such a good time," I said as we got to my house.

"Me, too. You're a lot of fun to be with."

The way my drooping, frizzy hair and running eye

makeup looked didn't seem to matter as we kissed good-night in my doorway. I couldn't believe a kiss could feel that great.

"Good luck with your French presentation on Monday," Eric called over his shoulder, "and with your exams. If you get nervous, try to laugh at it to yourself. That helps me."

"Thanks for the advice. I really had a great time," I called back.

I was headed for my phone to call Michelle when Mom found me. "Carly, you're soaked. I'll get you a towel. I'm glad you didn't get home too late. Your father was a nervous wreck. At the first crack of thunder he was at the window, peering between the blinds, watching for you. You should have seen him race through the house so you wouldn't catch him when you got home."

I laughed, picturing the sight.

"He loves you a lot, you know."

"I know." I dripped into my parents' room to give him a kiss even though he was asleep. I think worry wears him out.

Back in my room Mom handed me a towel and I dried off. "So?" she asked.

"So what?"

"You know," she said.

"You mean my date? How was it?" I tried to keep a straight face and act as if I had no idea why she was in my room looking all ready for a mother/daughter talk. "He's fun," I said as we both curled up on my bed. "We had a real good time." I lay down, unfastened the straps, and handed Mom my damp brace to hang up to dry.

"I hope it dries by morning," she said, "or you'll have to stay in bed."

"What a pain that will be."

"I know, honey," she said, "but that should be your worst problem. Just be happy you can walk."

"To tell you the truth, I'll be happy when my French presentation is over and when I don't have to wear that dumb brace anymore. And when people stop telling me what my worst problem is and how happy I should be that I can walk. I still have to face that checkup. If that's okay, if I can walk without a brace or surgery, then, Mom, you're going to see what happy looks like."

"I'd like that," she said. "When you're happy, I'm happy. I love you very much, you know."

"I love you, too."

She rumpled my damp hair and we talked a bit more. Rather, she listened and I talked. I felt good sharing this moment with her. "Life is strange," I said. "You never know what's in store for you, do you?"

"No, you don't," she said as she got up from my bed. "You just have to deal with it as best you can. Now get some sleep."

"Could you hand me my phone and punch in Michelle's number for me?" I asked, since with my brace off I couldn't move from my flat position.

"Isn't it too late to call her?"

"It's never too late to call Michelle. She's sitting by her phone waiting for me to call."

Mom dialed the number and handed me the receiver. She threw me a kiss and left the room.

Tonight I got a busy signal. Strange, I thought. Michelle's family usually doesn't make or get calls after ten P.M. except if Michelle is talking to me. At first I thought my mom dialed the wrong number. Now what would I do? Dumb back! Why did I have to be braceless and helpless? I couldn't even reach over to punch in the correct buttons on the phone. I got so angry I tried to reach part of the way. I gave up when I almost knocked over my lamp.

I might as well be a baby in a crib dependent on my parents to take care of me, I thought. I wanted to do something for myself. On Monday I'll call the hospital to make my appointment for X rays. The thought of X rays gave me a chill. What if the X rays showed I need surgery? I pushed the thought aside and hung up the receiver. At least I could still manage that. I couldn't fall asleep. I felt happy, excited feelings about my date with Eric, and scared feelings about Monday's tests, my French presentation, and the X rays. Why did Michelle's line have to be busy just when I needed her? If it was the right number, who was she talking to after ten-thirty, anyway? Then I realized I'd ranked my important problems in order. Michelle's not answering her phone the moment I called wasn't top of the list as it might have been before my accident. I guess things take on a different perspective when you have a real crisis in your life. I thought myself right to sleep.

JUNE

Chapter Fourteen

Even the Queen of England
Goes to the Bathroom

The next day Michelle heard all about my date. "Why didn't you call when you got home?" she asked.

"I did. Your line was busy."

"You must have gotten the wrong number," she said.

At breakfast on Monday morning between sips of coffee Mom said, "Relax about your speech. A speech is just talking to people and people are human. Everyone, even the Queen of England, goes to the bathroom, just like the rest of us. Even your French teacher, Mrs. Larson, is human. Remember that and you'll give a great presentation."

I was still trying to make sense out of Mom's advice when Dad added, "Picture yourself in front of the class confidently giving a great speech. That's called imaging."

"How come you didn't 'image' me coming home safely in spite of the storm last night?" I teased.

"I tried and it did help. Maybe it takes more practice when it involves your child's safety."

"Maybe," I said.

"Good luck," he added.

"Thanks. I'm glad you're getting help with your anxiety."

The doorbell rang. I gathered my books together and went to greet Michelle.

"You look great," she said, admiring my new pastel print skirt with a matching vest that covered my brace lumps. "How about practicing your French speech in the car?" she suggested.

At the mere mention of it, even on this hot day, I felt my hands get ice-cold. If I felt this anxious at home with family and friends, what would I feel like when I was standing in front of the class and Mme. Larson? The thought made my stomach act as if I'd taken an elevator ride from the top of the Empire State Building and come to a sudden stop.

"Don't worry," Michelle said. "You'll do fine. You'll see. Write me notes during the day. It'll keep you busy so you won't worry as much about tests and your speech."

I practiced my speech in the car in front of Mom, Michelle, Andrea, and Samantha.

"Best speech I ever heard," Andrea said, and Samantha agreed.

"That's great," I said, "except you two take Spanish and you don't understand a word of French."

"True, but we have good imaginations," Samantha answered.

"Your speech sounded good, although my French is rather rusty," Mom interrupted. "This has nothing to do with your speech, but before I forget . . . I called the hospital and made your X-ray appointment for Friday, late afternoon, so we can continue on to the lake. And Monday morning Dr. Ginario will check you over."

"You're leaving for the summer already?" Michelle said.

"Looks that way," I said, feeling annoyed. "You could have checked with me, Ma. Maybe I have plans. You didn't even ask."

"Carly, you always love going up to the lake for the summer. You're usually packed and ready to go before school is even over," Mom said.

"That was before Eric," Samantha said.

"I'm sorry," Mom said. "I didn't realize. If I thought you'd be upset, I never would have mentioned it— especially now, before your speech and the bio test."

"And Mom, Dr. Ginario told *me* to call for an appointment."

"But you haven't called," she answered. "I know you have a lot on your mind. I thought I'd help you out and do it for you."

My friends were all silent. I was embarrassed and anxious. I needed to feel grown-up and in control today more than ever. Instead I felt even more like a baby.

Finally, Mom came to a halt in front of school. "Good luck, sweetie. Don't be upset with me." She reached for my hand and held it until I said, "Okay," and got out.

There was a kind of energy in the halls that comes with the last week of classes. The air seemed to vibrate as kids talked full speed about how little they knew and how scared they were about exams. Usually I'm pretty confident, but since I'd missed three weeks of school, I felt more nervous and unsure than I'd ever been before. Today, at the thought of my speech, my stomach did not one but double and triple flips.

I looked around for Eric, but I didn't see him. Then he snuck up behind me, putting his hands over my eyes without saying a word. I knew by the way my heart beat that it was him, and I felt happy. I took his two hands in mine and leaned back against him. He quickly kissed the back of my head.

"Hi!" he said. "Ready for your big day? You look great."

"Hi," I answered, turning to face him. "I am really scared. It's summer and my teeth are chattering."

"I'll be thinking of you," Eric said as he walked Michelle and me to the elevator where Harris Walsh was waiting.

"Hi," Eric said to Harris. "Are you going to camp this summer?"

"Just for the second month," Harris answered, "after my cast comes off."

"Hope we're in the same bunk again," Eric said, and Michelle's jaw dropped open. I probably had a surprised look on my face, too. Eric knew Harris well. That was news to me.

"If the elevator gets stuck, take good care of my girlfriend, Carly. And of course her friend Michelle," Eric said, sort of introducing us to Harris. I nearly flipped at his words. I was actually a girlfriend in his mind. Wow!

"Sure," Harris said.

The door closed as Eric called, "Good luck, Carly."

Then Harris Walsh, who's barely said two words to

us the entire time I've been back, turned into the friendliest guy.

"I didn't know you were going with Eric," he said to me.

"We just went to the movies."

He didn't even hear my answer. He was staring at Michelle. I thought she'd faint when he asked her, "Are you going with anyone?"

"Not at the moment," she answered.

"Maybe the four of us could go out sometime, or are you both going to camp for the summer?" Harris added.

"I'll be going up to our lake house on Friday, after finals," I said.

"I'll be in the city for most of the summer," Michelle said.

"What's your number?" Harris asked. "I'll give you a call."

Michelle whipped out a pen and wrote her name and number on his book cover.

The elevator stopped at the fourth floor. Harris went off in one direction and Michelle and I went off in the other.

Michelle gave my arm a squeeze that I'm sure left fingerprints. "Was I dreaming," she asked, "or did that conversation really take place?"

"I'm your witness. It definitely took place." I smiled at her and added, "He finally sees the light and notices how terrific you are."

"It's more likely I'm the only girl who's going to be in the city in July."

"You have to learn to take a compliment," I said, "and not be so down on yourself."

"Who are you, the school psychologist?" Michelle joked. "Ever since you came home from the hospital you know all the answers."

"No, I was just remembering something my hospital friend Tina said, and I'm passing it on to you. By the way, since when does one date mean I'm going with someone?"

At the door to my bio class I took my books from Michelle.

"Good luck," she said. "I'll keep my fingers crossed that your speech goes well in French."

"Thanks. I need all the help I can get."

I tried not to think about French and just deal with the bio test. One thing I'd learned for sure over the past month was to take one step at a time. Maybe it wouldn't be hard, I hoped. I glanced at the copy on my desk. No such luck. I tried to think of something to make me laugh at it and relax, as Eric had suggested. I pictured Tina, Jess, and me the last night we were in the hospital together. Each of us tried to make the others laugh by telling our favorite jokes. Tina would mess up the punch line and say, "Well, it's funny when Leo tells it." The expression on her face had been funnier than the joke. The three of us together, laughing, was a memory I'd never forget, even if I never saw them again. I struggled through the exam and handed the paper in early so I wouldn't start changing possible right answers to probable wrong ones.

Then, with time to kill, I wrote a note to Michelle. I

didn't want to think about French and start my head pounding. I wrote:

> Michelle,
> Hi! How are you? Still thinking about (?) and hoping he'll call? I know he will. I just finished a really hard bio test. I got really scared. I tried to do what (!) said, laugh at it, but it didn't work.
> My hair is *so* frizzy! I wish it didn't look so bad, especially today. I can't believe (!) called me his girlfriend after one date. He never asked me to go steady. Maybe I would, but maybe I wouldn't now that I'm going up to the lake. You never can tell who you're going to meet up there, if you know what I mean. Gotta go.
>
> C.

I folded up the note and handed it to Michelle as we passed each other in the hall. She handed me a note, too. I didn't have time to read it in French, my next class. My heart beat louder each step closer I got. I could hear it and wondered if anyone else heard it, too. My knees were turning to mush and the vein on the side of my forehead was throbbing. I felt as if I'd throw up if I stepped into the room. I tried stepping in, took two steps, turned, and raced down the hall to the girls' room. This had never happened to me before.

As I stood by the sink, putting cold water on my

face, I looked up into the mirror above. The color and expression on my face made me immediately think of the way my father looked when he tried to come into my hospital room. I thought about his "anxiety group" and what he's learned. "Anxiety is caused by an overload of stress." I repeated his words to calm myself. So this was how he must have felt when I was in the hospital. Pretty awful. I felt guilty. I wished I'd understood him better.

I tried to think only positive thoughts. Words such as Jess's always calling me a winner. I thought about Tina's positive attitude about life, and then I tried out my father's method of imaging. I pictured myself in front of my French class confidently giving the best speech even Mme. Larson ever heard. My heart started beating normally again. My hands stopped sweating. As I got more and more ready to face what I had to do, I realized my father wasn't weak just because he had a problem. I could see how courageous he really was. His being honest and sharing with me step by step what he was doing to overcome his fear taught me to be braver. I strode confidently into my French class.

"We gave up on you, Carly," Mme. Larson said. "We thought you fell in." The class laughed at her joke as they were expected to.

I didn't laugh or explain anything. I just put my books down, took my speech out, and stood in front of the class. I looked around, remembering to think how everyone in this room is human, and to appear as if I didn't have an ounce of fear. Of course, no one could see my legs shaking as I gave my speech.

I'm sure about a third of the class didn't understand a word I said, but they weren't about to let Mme. Larson know that, so those kids mumbled "Great speech" and "Good job" along with the others as I walked down the aisle to my seat. Mme. Larson, on the other hand, corrected words I'd mispronounced.

At the end of class, Mme. Larson called me over. I thought she remembered a few more words I misused or messed up on.

"Don't you feel proud of yourself?" she said. "In this class you were treated like everyone else and you didn't have time to feel sorry for yourself. You got an A, by the way."

"I do feel proud of myself, Mme. Larson, and I appreciate your treating me like everyone else," I said. Then I took a deep breath and risked losing my A to add, "But I think you could treat everyone in the class a little more kindly." I wasn't sure where the courage to say that came from, and I said it very sweetly, without any anger or freshness in my voice.

Mme. Larson looked back at her papers. "I've learned to work through thick or thin. It takes your mind off your pain. That will be all," she said without further explanation. She didn't have to say anything else. Now I felt terrific.

Eric was waiting for me in the hall.

"I heard from the other kids in the class that you were great! But then, I already knew that." He put his arm around my waist and left it there as we walked to my next class.

131

When I got to my seat, I opened the note from Michelle. I read:

Hi

If you read this before your speech, good luck. You can do it!

If you read this after your speech, congratulations! I'm sure you did a great job!

I can't believe you'll be going off to the lake so soon, especially now with Harris going to call me. I'm not ready to say good-bye, and it makes me worry to think about you up there. I hope your X rays are okay. I'll never forgive myself if they're not.

M.

I felt good having friends like Eric and Michelle so confident in me. I also felt worried about Michelle. I noticed that she handles crises by feeling guilty. Then I realized that's her way. But it didn't have to be mine. We didn't think the same way about romance either anymore. I wished I could help her feel better. I wished I could help Mom, Dad, and Pam feel better, too. I wondered, was anyone wishing the same for me? It wasn't my fault they felt guilty. I got a lonely feeling inside as if all the emotions I'd buried were letting me know they were still there.

Chapter Fifteen

From Something Bad
Comes Something Good

Eric came to my house on Thursday night. "I love when finals are over," I said to him.

"My last one today was tough, but I think I did okay," he said, and followed me to my room. "Nice room. I know there must be a chair somewhere under these clothes."

"Here," I said, taking an armful of blouses off the rocker in the corner of my room.

He watched me pack up for my summer at the lake. "Do you know you have twenty-five belts?" he asked as I put one last one in a carton from my father's store.

"Different colors," I said. "You don't outgrow belts. They seem to multiply in the drawer."

"Guys live a full and complete life with maybe three belts, tops," Eric said, then suddenly got serious. He got up from the rocking chair and sat down next to me on my bed. He folded up sweaters and handed them to me. "I'll miss you, Carly. I really will. I usually love going to camp. I've got a lot of friends there, and I've looked forward to being a junior counselor this summer. But I'd rather be with you."

I wanted to say, I miss you and you're not even gone yet, but I guess his words sounded so grown-up and sincere that I got too scared to answer back my real feelings. Instead I said, "You'll love camp once you're there with your friends again. And we can write lots of letters to each other."

"I'll write you every day and twice on Sunday," he said.

"Agreed."

"Hope you can read my handwriting."

"I'm good at figuring out handwriting. Don't worry. I'll read every letter at least twice, okay?"

"Okay," he said. "I wish I could stay longer, but I have to work at the pharmacy again tonight." He got up and so did I. We hugged tightly while saying good-bye.

"Look at the full moon tonight. Wherever we are, we'll see the same moon," I said, not even caring if I sounded corny.

Then Eric kissed me for a long time. It felt so good. I think we both didn't want it to end. When the kiss was over, Eric put his hands on my shoulders and said, "Ten o'clock every night, look at the moon and think of me, and I'll be looking at the same moon thinking of you."

Now that's what I call really romantic and private. As I walked Eric to the door, his arm was around my waist. My brace got in the way of my feeling his touch until he let his hand slip down a bit to my hip. At the doorway he turned me toward him and put his other hand on my other hip. Then we kissed good-bye and I waved till he was out of sight. I felt almost homesick. I went back to my room, closed the door, and lay down on my bed burying my head in my pillow. I just lay there, not moving until Mom called, "Michelle's here!" I hadn't even heard the doorbell ring.

"Come in," I called, answering the knock at my bedroom door.

Michelle opened the door slowly and peeked in. Then she sort of floated over to my bed as if her feet hardly touched the ground. "Guess who phoned me?" she said.

"Harris called you already? The boy doesn't waste any time. Hugging her, I said, "I'm so happy for you."

"I don't believe it." She squealed and pounded my bed with her fists. "He asked me out a week from Saturday. He's busy this weekend with visiting relatives. What am I going to wear?"

"Where are you going?"

"Good question. I don't know. We didn't decide yet."

"Then you have nothing to worry about yet."

"This is true," she said. "But you won't be here next weekend to help me decide. You'll be at the lake. Carly, I hate saying good-bye to you when summer comes and your room looks like this, your clothes packed in cartons."

"I don't like saying good-bye to you, either, especially this summer. For some reason I'm having a really tough time with good-byes. Wait a minute," I said, getting a great idea. "Maybe we just need a little more time together because we missed it when I was in the hospital. Why don't you come up to the lake with me for this first week? We can pick up where we left off."

Michelle got pale. "I don't think I want to. It has too many bad memories. And what if you get hurt again because of me?"

"I didn't get hurt because of you. I got hurt because of me." I lowered my voice. "But I think I know how you feel. I love it there, and yet I sort of feel afraid to go back to the spot at the lake where the accident happened. Maybe if we did it together, it would help both of us?" I could hear a sound of pleading in my voice that surprised me. I thought I was doing this for Michelle . . . to help her, but as I spoke I realized maybe I needed her there to help me.

"Go ask your mom and then I'll ask mine," Michelle said, brightening a bit as she started to help me. "I'll be there with you."

I was glad when our parents thought it was a great idea. Michelle went home to pack.

The next afternoon, as I waited for Mom to pick up Michelle and me, I looked out the window. I saw a neighbor wheeling a stroller with a baby in it. "I just love babies. Maybe I'll be an aunt one of these days if Pam and Warren work out their problems," I said.

"What's happening with them?" Michelle asked.

"We don't exactly know. Pam wrote that she doesn't want to make an issue of discussing personal marriage business with every member of her family. Warren gets upset with that. They're seeing a marriage counselor, though. We're all dying to know what's going on, but afraid to ask."

Mom's horn signaled her arrival as we grabbed Michelle's suitcase and my cartons and loaded up the car.

"Wait till you see the new store," Mom said proudly as we drove toward it. "Your father's been real busy setting it up, but it was worth it. I'm glad he's taking the weekend off. We could both use the rest."

Dad looked so happy as he greeted us and showed us around. "I thought it was the end of the world to have to move to a new store," he said, "but from something bad came something good. A bigger store and new customers in addition to the regulars who haven't dropped us."

"So many racks of clothes," I said.

"It's great," Michelle said.

"You sure did a good job," I added.

"It was no easy task. But your father is terrific. Did you know that?" Mom gave him a kiss on the lips, not even caring that Michelle was here with me.

"I couldn't have done it without your support, sweetie," Dad said, and kissed her back.

"That's very romantic, the way your folks kiss and talk to each other," Michelle whispered to me.

"We'd better get on our way to the hospital so Carly doesn't miss her appointment," Mom reminded us.

At her words Dad's expression changed. He got jittery and beads of sweat appeared on his forehead.

I didn't feel angry or annoyed this time. I thought about how I'd felt before giving my French speech. I reached over and took his hand. "It'll be all right. You'll see," I comforted him. "Image it," I added. "It helped me, with my speech."

"I'm glad to hear I helped you," Dad said.

A little later, on the way to the hospital, we were all quiet in the car. Maybe we were all busy imaging. Who knows? I took my mind off my nervousness by listening to the music and picturing being with Eric.

We pulled up at the hospital right on schedule. I felt quivery inside, like I'd swallowed a frog or something. Don't lose it now, I told myself. Hang on a bit longer. I thought the words to myself, but this time they weren't working as well. I wondered if my nervousness was causing my back to ache.

"You don't all have to go in with me," I said.

"I'll go with you," Michelle said, and we both started to get out of the car.

I heard my dad take a deep breath and let it out slowly. "Give us a minute or so and we'll be in, too," he said.

"Take your time," I said. "I can handle this." I've handled every unexpected twist and turn in my life lately, I thought. Why did I have this uneasy feeling now, like I had to get it all out. I didn't know how much longer I could hang on—or even if I wanted to. I squeezed Michelle's hand as we walked inside pushing the heavy glass of the doors.

The odor of disinfectant and the memories of loneliness and fear hit me immediately. What if my X rays weren't good? What if I needed surgery? What if there was more damage and I wasn't allowed to go home like last time? I could feel my heart pounding inside my chest.

"It'll be okay, you'll see," Michelle comforted me. I was sure she could feel my palms sweating.

I checked in at the X-ray department. I saw people in wheelchairs waiting their turn while holding ice-packs on ankles or wrists.

"We're going to have a long wait," I said to Michelle after checking with a technician. "Let's go visit my old floor and see if Judy is around. Sitting here is driving me crazy."

As the elevator doors opened and we started to enter, I heard my mother call to me, "Carly, where are you going?"

I looked in the direction of her voice and saw her hand in hand with my father, inching their way slowly toward us.

"You're doing great, Dad. I love you," I said. "There's a delay for X rays. We'll be back in fifteen minutes. We're going visiting. I need to move around right now."

At the nurses' station on my floor I approached Mrs. Todd, expecting her to recognize me. I thought she would ask if I was visiting from Europe since this wasn't visiting hours.

She stared at me blankly as if she'd never seen me before and asked, "Yes. Can I help you?"

Maybe I looked different in jeans with zippers on the legs and socks up over the bottoms. Maybe if I wore a hospital gown instead of my long blouse, or was lying down with a sheet covering half of me, she'd remember me.

"It's me, Carly, the girl with the broken back. Is Judy here today?"

"Well, look at you, Carly. You look so rosy-cheeked and healthy now." She almost sounded as if she cared, I thought.

"Judy," she called to a figure scurrying into a nearby room. "We have a visitor."

"I actually think Mrs. Todd thinks I came back to say hello to her," I whispered to Michelle.

Judy greeted me with a hug. "I've wondered how you were getting along," she said.

"I'll know better after my X rays," I said. "Did you ever hear from Jess or Tina?"

"Yes, I did see Jess," Judy said. "He asked me about you, just like you asked me about him. Of course I didn't have anything to tell him because you never did write to me, you know."

"I'm sorry," I said. "I meant to. I was just so busy."

"That's okay. Just teasing. It happens all the time. People are very close in hospitals, but when they get out, they don't have much to say to each other anymore."

"Judy, this is my best friend, Michelle." I apologized for being rude.

"Glad to meet you, Michelle," Judy said.

"I heard from Tina a while ago but not recently. Heard from her lately?" I asked again.

"I don't know anything more about Tina, which is good news, because it means she didn't end up back here again."

"Carly, we'd better get back for your X rays," Michelle reminded me, and my stomach flipped again.

Judy and I hugged good-bye. "As much as I like both you and Dr. Ginario, I hope I don't end up back here again."

"Good luck with your X rays," Judy said, and walked me to the elevator.

"I'll need it," I said. As the elevator started down, my knees began to tremble again. If ever I needed a philosophy—or a prayer—it was now.

Chapter Sixteen

What Will Be Will Be

"I have to wait until Monday for Dr. Ginario to tell me the results," I said to my folks and Michelle when I returned to the waiting room after my X rays.

"A whole weekend of waiting?" Dad said.

"We'll all have to be patient and keep ourselves busy. Some prayers wouldn't hurt, either," Mom added.

"I've been patient," I said as we walked out of the hospital. "Very patient. I don't know if I can last the weekend." Michelle and I walked on ahead. I felt so glad she was here with me.

Usually I get happier as I get near the lake. Tonight part of me was dreading it. Mom and Dad were too busy with the new store for weekends away, so we hadn't been back since the accident. Now as we got closer, my strong feelings surprised me. I couldn't bury my nervousness. I wanted to run alongside the car rather than ride in it. I felt like a pot of spaghetti just before it boils over. The familiar sound of gravel crunching under the tires as we pulled into the driveway made me think of our speedy getaway to the hospital almost two months ago. I could feel my heart pounding. Dad turned the motor off and everyone looked at me.

"What are you all looking at?" I said sharply. "I'm okay. I'm fine."

"You don't sound okay," Michelle said.

She was right. "Okay, I'm angry!" I said. "For a few minutes I just need to worry about myself."

"Can I do anything for you?" Dad asked as I bounded out of the car. "Where are you going?"

"I'm going down to the lake—I don't want to, but I need to now," I said.

"Why?" Mom asked. "It can wait until tomorrow. We're all tired now."

I never knew how powerful feelings could be or how strong they become when you bury them.

"I'm tired of waiting for the right moment to express my feelings. Maybe I don't even have any feelings left!" I screamed, and started to run.

"Carly, be careful!" Mom shouted. "The ground is uneven and it's getting dark."

"Walk," Dad commanded.

Their words made me run faster. I didn't even slow down when Michelle shouted, "Wait for me."

But she did catch up. "Watch your step." Her voice trembled. "Don't get hurt again. Please slow down... do it for me."

It was as if her words, along with the panicked sound of my parents' footsteps, triggered a feeling deep inside me. "I can't think about anyone's feelings or problems right now. I need to be alone. I've held in all my feelings for too long. I can't do it anymore. You have no idea what it's like to be scared that I'll need—surgery—or how I felt when I thought I wouldn't walk again."

I was standing where the hammock cord had broken and I'd fallen. I felt as if the memory knocked the wind out of me again. I knelt down on the damp ground and smacked at it with my hands like a two-year-old whose mother takes it to the spot where it got hurt. Tears were streaming down my cheeks.

Mom and Michelle tried to stop me, but Dad said, "Let her be. She's got to let her feelings out in her own way. We all react differently. We do what we have to do."

Michelle was crying, too. "I'm sorry," she said. "Please don't cry anymore."

"I know you're sorry. That's not the point. Can't you just see there's a crisis going on right now."

She got down on the ground with me and put her arms around me. Her comforting touch was better than any words she could have said.

"I understand," Mom whispered, and stroked my head. "I understand how bad you feel. How scared, too. You've been through an awful time." For the first time she didn't say *we've* been through an awful time or it should be your worst problem.

Dad got down with us, too. "You've been very brave, too brave," he said. "You've been so concerned with all our individual crises that you buried your own. But we all deal with crises in our own way. My way was very obvious. Do you know what your mother did?"

"What?" I said. Mom had seemed so cool and collected during the past weeks, as if she alone were keeping the lid on the entire family.

"Tell her," Dad said, "what you did first when you got back from the hospital the day she was hurt."

"I wouldn't talk to anyone," Mom said, stroking my hair as she spoke. "I went right to the drawer in the kitchen where I keep the heavy-duty scissors, and I took them down to the lake and sat in the dark for an hour till I cut up the entire hammock and threw the pieces in the garbage pail. I couldn't keep anything in the house that hurt my child!"

"You destroyed the hammock?" I said, amazed. "You're the one who is always in control."

"I wasn't being rational," Mom went on. "I was just reacting in my own way. I was terrified, but I wanted to be calm to help you two." She put her arms around me and my father. "Cutting up the hammock was the only thing in my control. It may have been a little crazy, but I'm not sorry I did it. I felt better. It helped me so I could help you."

I leaned back against Mom's shoulder and took a deep breath. I let it out slowly like my father does, and the feeling of waves in my stomach lessened. I guess we'd all handled our problems in our own way.

Michelle was sitting on the ground nearby, very quiet, shivering. I reached over for her hand. "I'm sorry I screamed at all of you. I really lost it, didn't I?" I said. "I don't like to act that way."

"Guess what?" Dad said. "You're not perfect and neither are we. But we all love each other and are here to support and accept each other...as is, and that's what counts." He leaned over and kissed the top of my head.

"Do you think even the Queen of England goes to pieces now and then?" I asked Mom, and she laughed.

We all sat quietly together, watching the moon appear. I thought of Eric and knew that at ten that night we'd both be looking at this same moon. Maybe Eric would never have asked me out again after I turned him down if it hadn't been for my broken back. I don't know the why of things, but the closeness I felt with my family and Michelle helped me think clearly. Spending the weekend getting crazy with worry didn't make much sense.

"What will be will be," I said out loud, as if the answer had come to me. "Let's have the best weekend ever. Every day has little or big crises. I can't be so busy worrying about them all that I forget to notice the happy moments in the same day."

"When did you become a philosopher?" Dad asked.

"It's a little something that I picked up from a friend in the hospital." I felt so much better with my feelings out in the open. It amazed me.

On Sunday night, Michelle and I carefully polished our toenails a different color on each nail.

On Monday when Dr. Ginario examined me and gave me the good news, I wiggled my toes like mad and he laughed at the sight.

"You've healed very well," he said. "You won't need surgery. Any questions?"

No surgery. I breathed the biggest sigh of relief.

"Do I have to wear my brace anymore? Can I swim? Can I go in the motorboat?" I felt so much happiness thinking about the things I love to do and would soon get to do again, I could even wait patiently while Dr. Ginario checked my records. Somehow I felt I could handle whatever would come next. Maybe going through a crisis made me stronger. I felt more grown-up knowing what's really a serious problem. Things that used to bother me like frizzy hair or broken nails or too much homework were just not that important anymore. Finally Dr. Ginario answered my questions.

"In three more weeks you can be braceless and carefree, swim and go boating. Just take it slowly."

Before I got dressed, I scribbled a note and sent it "by nurse" to my parents. I wrote, "Dear Mom and Dad, Don't worry. I'm fine."

My parents and Michelle were overjoyed with the good news. I cried with happiness as we left the office. Michelle whispered, "I'm sorry it ever happened."

"I've healed," I said to Michelle, "but you haven't. How can I help you?"

"Just get better and always be my friend," she said as we walked to the car.

I made a formal oath I knew I'd never break. "I, Carly Stern, age thirteen, will fully recover and always be your friend. That's for sure."

Michelle smiled and squeezed my hand.

As we rode through town I looked around. Since my accident I was aware that I was realizing more and more interesting things about life.

"Carly, I just asked you something. What are you

thinking about so hard that you didn't even hear me?" Michelle said.

"I was just wondering about my old friends from the hospital—Tina and Jess. It's true everywhere you go that some people you care about you may never see again, especially if you met in a hospital."

"I never really thought about it," Michelle said.

"You sound so much more mature, Carly," Mom said, and smiled. Dad nodded, obviously agreeing with Mom.

They should only realize how far I've come, I thought. I finally accepted that people love each other in different ways and have to accept their differences. I have expectations, but I also know not to expect the impossible of my family, Michelle, Eric, other people I don't even know yet... and myself.

"Earth to Carly, come in, Carly!" Michelle got my attention again. "Now what are you thinking?"

"My body's healing helped all of us to grow," I said, trying to be matter-of-fact.

"That's an interesting insight," Dad said.

I can't say I'm glad I had to go through all this, but at least I learned a lot.

I think every now and then, even when I get older, I'll wiggle my toes to remind me what's important. Of course when I get older, I may not remember. Will I remember? I'll have to wait and see, I guess. Life's funny that way.

ABOUT THE AUTHOR

CAROL SNYDER was born and raised in Brooklyn, New York. She is the author of several widely acclaimed books for children and young adults, including *Memo to Myself When I Have a Teenage Kid*, *The Leftover Kid*, and *Leave Me Alone, Ma*, an IRA / CBC Children's Choice Award winner and an *American Bookseller* Pick of the List. A former teacher, Mrs. Snyder now writes full time. She lives in Bridgewater, New Jersey, with her husband. They have two daughters.

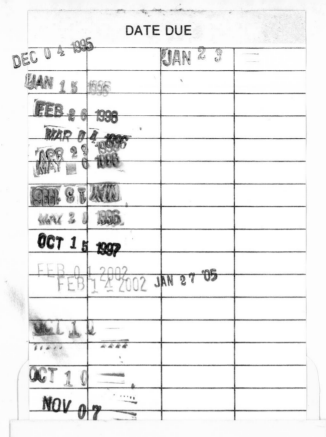

DATE DUE

DEC 0 4 1995		JAN 2 3	
JAN 1 5 1996			
FEB 2 6 1996			
MAR 0 4 1996			
APR 2 9 1996			
MAY 0 6 1996			
JAN 8 1996			
MAY 2 0 1996			
OCT 1 5 1997			
FEB 0 1 2002	FEB 1 4 2002	JAN 27 '05	
OCT 1 0			
OCT 1 0			
NOV 0 7			